Could it really be him?

It had been almost four years. All they'd shared was one night. Or was it two? Or three? Or more? Orla wished she could remember, but her memory had as many holes in it as a lump of Swiss cheese.

"Mummy!"

Her son's voice broke through the fog of fear in her head.

Stretching her cheeks into a smile, she finally had a clear view past her sister to the spot at the left of the altar where she'd been promised she and Finn would sit.

The smile froze, half-formed.

A tall, dark, utterly gorgeous man sat beside Finn. His black stare was fixed directly on her.

Her stomach plummeted. Thick heat pulsed and swirled through her head, dizzying her.

The man watching over her son until she could take her place beside him was Tonino. Finn's father.

Michelle Smart's love affair with books started when she was a baby, when she would cuddle them in her cot. A voracious reader of all genres, she found her love of romance established when she stumbled across her first Harlequin book at the age of twelve. She's been reading—and writing—them ever since. Michelle lives in Northamptonshire, England, with her husband and two young Smarties.

Visit the Author Profile page at Harlequin.com for more titles.

Michelle Smart

—

HER SICILIAN BABY REVELATION

HARLEQUIN
PRESENTS

HARLEQUIN®
PRESENTS®

Recycling programs
for this product may
not exist in your area.

ISBN-13: 978-1-335-89343-7

Her Sicilian Baby Revelation

Copyright © 2020 by Michelle Smart

All rights reserved. No part of this book may be used or reproduced in
any manner whatsoever without written permission except in the case of
brief quotations embodied in critical articles and reviews.

This is a work of fiction. Names, characters, places and incidents
are either the product of the author's imagination or are used fictitiously.
Any resemblance to actual persons, living or dead, businesses,
companies, events or locales is entirely coincidental.

This edition published by arrangement with Harlequin Books S.A.

For questions and comments about the quality of this book,
please contact us at CustomerService@Harlequin.com.

Harlequin Enterprises ULC
22 Adelaide St. West, 40th Floor
Toronto, Ontario M5H 4E3, Canada
www.Harlequin.com

Printed in U.S.A.

HER SICILIAN BABY REVELATION

This book is dedicated to my munchkin Zak xxx

PROLOGUE

ORLA O'REILLY BLEW her nose and swallowed back a breath, trying her hardest to stop fresh tears falling down her sodden cheeks. She didn't want people to see her like this.

She'd flown to Sicily ten days ago on a mission to meet the man her mother had always unkindly referred to as 'Orla's sperm donor'. Only now did she understand her mother had actually been diplomatic.

Her father, who'd returned from his travels that morning, had refused to see her. He had no curiosity about his twenty-three-year-old daughter. No curiosity at all.

She hadn't expected a grand reunion or anything but his outright rejection…

It hurt. Really, really hurt. Now all she wanted was Tonino's strong arms holding her tightly and his breath whispering into her hair that everything would be okay.

At least something good had come from her time in Sicily. She'd met the man of her dreams.

Ten days ago she'd taken one look at her room in the budget hotel she'd checked into and gone back to the reception. Orla was not one for complaining but the state of it would have driven a saint to boiling point. The bed sheets were stained and crumpled, the carpet sticky under her feet and the bathroom…well, the less said about that, the better.

She'd stood at that reception desk for exactly six minutes before a tall, imposing figure had appeared from a door marked *Privato* and Orla had found herself face-to-face with the sexiest man she'd ever set eyes on.

Until that first sight of Tonino, she'd never understood what it meant to meet someone and feel as if you'd been struck by lightning.

When she'd returned to the hotel much later that day, her first attempt to meet her father scuppered due to him being abroad, she'd found her room hadn't just been cleaned but sanitised. New furniture and furnishings had been installed, including a brand-new carpet. Her melancholy mood had lifted when the gorgeous hotel manager had knocked on the door and asked if she would like to meet for coffee in the morning.

What had followed had been the most wonderful week and a half of her life, right until two hours ago when she'd returned to her father's home for her second attempt. All those glorious hours with Tonino had infused her with a sense of optimism. She had become certain that her first meeting with her father would be the stuff of Hollywood; all tight embraces and schmaltzy words.

It had taken her father exactly eight minutes to break her heart, the length of time his housekeeper had made Orla wait alone on the doorstep before she'd returned with the 'regretful' news that he didn't want to meet her.

She must try not to think about her father. Keep her focus on Tonino.

That was what she needed to keep the tears at bay. To think of the man who'd brought her to life and stolen her heart.

She wished she'd told him about her father. She wished she'd had the courage to be upfront about her real reason for being in Sicily but it was such a shameful thing to admit, that she was the secret love child of one of Sicily's most notorious playboys; a child created through infidelity.

All her life she'd shied away from meaningful friendships and relationships. The only people she'd ever trusted were her sister, Aislin, and her grandparents. Her grandparents had both since died so that left Aislin.

And then she'd met Tonino.

She was ready to tell him now. He would understand. He would comfort her. He would be the rock she'd always dreamed of having but had never believed could exist.

Tonino had left her in bed that morning with a lingering kiss. He'd stroked her cheek and promised that that night they would talk. The expression in his eyes and the tone of his voice had told her this would be of a serious nature. As hard as she tried to temper the wild emotions raging through her veins, not even her father's rejection could completely stamp them out. A future was dangling before her. For the first time in her life, Orla felt that her future could mean more than a career. It could involve…love…

The taxi driver pulled up outside her hotel behind a sparkling stretch limousine that stuck out like a sore thumb in this run-down area. Orla wearily slipped out, intent only on getting to her room and soaking in the bath while she waited for Tonino to return from his business trip in Tuscany. This was the first time they'd been apart for more than a few hours. How lucky was she to have found the man of her dreams just as he was due to take his annual leave, giving them all that time together!

'Permesso.'

A ravishing stick-thin blonde with eyes like a cat's blocked Orla's path to the hotel's elevator.

Orla held her hands up and tried to move around her, but the woman mimicked her moves, blocking her efforts.

'Can I help you?' The richness of the woman's clothes and the expert precision of her hair and make-up made Orla think she must be the possessor of the limousine.

The woman raised an immaculately plucked eyebrow. 'English?'

'Irish.'

'You give me two minutes.'

'Err…' Annoyed, Orla was about to push her way around the woman when the four fatal words were uttered.

'Is about Tonino Valente.'

Prickles raced up Orla's spine. Her abdomen clenched. 'What about him?'

The woman raised her left hand and pointed at her wedding finger. A huge diamond ring lay snugly on it. 'I am Sophia. Tonino's fiancée.'

Twenty minutes later and the two women were in Orla's hotel room. Sophia perched delicately on the small armchair while Orla sat on the floor feeling as if she'd been punched by a heavyweight with lead in his gloves. Spread on the carpet around her were photographs of Tonino and Sophia. Many photos. There were also press clippings and glossy magazines. Orla didn't understand Sicilian but some of the words in the article needed no translation. Tonino and Sophia's engagement party two months ago had been deemed newsworthy.

'I sorry to tell you this,' Sophia said in a tone that suggested she was loving every minute of it. 'Tonino has made fool of you. He has lied to you. You are fun to him. *Sì?*'

'I've been a bit of fun?' Orla whispered. 'Is that what you're saying?'

'*Sì.* That why I here. I warn you. Tonino loves me. We are to marry.'

Orla was unaware that tears were leaking down her face, and too numb to care that there was a warning in the Sicilian woman's tone as well as in her actual words.

This must be what he'd wanted to talk to her about that night.

Fool that she was, she'd believed he wanted to discuss a future for them.

Her hand shook as she picked up the glossy magazine containing a twenty-page spread of their engagement party.

How could an ordinary hotel manager attract

such a wealthy, high-maintenance woman like this? And why would an ordinary hotel manager be the recipient of the kind of press attention usually reserved for the rich and famous?

Fearing she could be sick, she groped for her phone and keyed Tonino Valente's name into the search engine.

Ten minutes later she was still reading and searching but it was as if someone had taken possession of her body and was reading the damning evidence for her.

She felt light-headed. Boneless.

Tonino had lied about more than his marital status.

He wasn't the manager of the hotel as he'd led her to believe. He was the owner. This hotel was just a small cog in a vast empire.

Tonino Valente was the sole owner of Valente Holdings, a chain of mostly hugely expensive hotels across Europe that catered for the filthy rich. Tonino, who was also an enthusiastic investor in start-up businesses, was filthy rich in his own right.

The man she'd opened her heart for, who she'd dared believe she could have a future with, was a cheat and a liar. The worst kind of liar. A rich, powerful liar. His grandfather was one of Sicily's top judges. His mother was one of Sicily's leading criminal lawyers. His father was a leading Sicilian politician.

Her Internet search revealed that the immaculately beautiful woman in the obscenely expensive outfit sitting on Orla's hotel-room armchair was Sophia Messina. The Messinas were a Sicilian family as wealthy and powerful as the Valentes.

'I'm sorry,' she whispered, meeting Sophia's cold, unflinching eyes. 'I knew nothing about you.'

'Now you know...you go?' It was framed as a question, but the underlying threat hung between them.

Orla didn't need the threat.

'Yes.' Breathing heavily to quell the rising nausea, she stumbled over to the wardrobe. 'Yes. I go.'

CHAPTER ONE

Four years later

'WILL YOU KEEP still a minute?' Orla rebuked with a shake of her head. How was she supposed to fasten her sister's wedding dress if she didn't stop jigging on the spot?

'I'm *trying*,' Aislin protested.

'Try harder. These clasps are fiddly. Breathe in.'

Aislin gave a theatrical intake of breath.

Using all her limited strength, Orla hooked the second tiny clasp. Excellent. Only another fifteen of the blasted things to go. 'Are you sure you don't want to wear a bra?'

'It's a strapless dress.'

'Then wear a strapless bra. What will you do if the dress falls down and your boobs start wobbling for all of Sicily's high society to admire?' If there was one thing Orla was envious of, it was her sister's magnificent bosom. Orla barely had a handful to waste.

'It's a bespoke dress. It's not going to fall down.'

She hooked the third clasp. 'I don't get why you won't let the designer hoist you into it.'

'She's around if we need her.'

'But she's used to doing this. Her fingers work. My fingers are *useless*.' Fourth hook clasped, Orla blew out a puff of air from the exertion.

'Untwist your knickers and chill. Anyone would think you were the one getting married.'

'Aren't you the slightest bit nervous?'

'Nope.' Through the reflection of the full-length mirror, Orla saw the beaming smile spread over her sister's face. And well she should smile. Not only was Aislin marrying the love of her life, but she'd discovered a month ago that she was pregnant.

That the man Orla's sister was marrying happened to be Orla's half-brother—Orla and Aislin had different fathers—was, to her mind, only further cause for celebration.

She just wished they were marrying in Ireland, not here in Sicily. She was certain the deterioration in her coordination was down to the knots of dread in her stomach. Or were they knots of excitement?

All she knew for certain was that the beats of her heart had steadily increased in tempo and density in the weeks leading up to the wedding and now that she was finally in Sicily, there was an anticipation…or dread…that something was going to happen.

It was close to four years since Orla had been in Sicily on her futile mission to meet her father. A serious car accident six months after her return to Ireland had left her with major memory problems. Time had healed most of the holes in her memory but the period from Sicily to the accident itself remained stubbornly locked away.

She knew her wish to meet her father had gone unfulfilled only because Aislin had told her so and because every time Orla thought of Salvatore Moncada she wanted to cry. She'd shed a bucket of tears when she'd learned he'd died a year ago but even during that mammoth crying session was the feeling that she was crying for more than the father she'd never met.

She comforted herself that she'd gained a brother, Salvatore's son, Dante. He was technically a half-brother, as Aislin was technically her half-sister, but Orla had never been able to see it like that. You didn't love someone in halves. You either loved them or you didn't. Aislin was only three years younger than her so she had no memories of life without her. Aislin was her sister and they would fight to the death to protect each other.

Dante, who Aislin had found for Orla and

fallen in love with for herself, had only been in their lives for four months but it felt as if he'd been a part of it for ever.

Aislin's phone buzzed. 'Can you get that?'

'Okay, but don't move. If the clasps pop open I'm not redoing them.' She still had a dozen of the ruddy things left to hook together.

She strode to the suite's dressing table, grabbed the phone, handed it to Aislin and then got back to work on the dress.

'It's a message from our dear mother.' Aislin spoke in an unnaturally high voice.

A shiver ran up Orla's spine and her fingers fumbled on the delicate clasp she'd only just gripped hold of. 'What does she want?'

'To wish me luck.'

She snorted. 'How big of her.'

'Now, now, don't be like that. You know it isn't easy to jump on a plane to be there for your youngest daughter's wedding.'

'True. It's not as if her daughter's fiancé is a billionaire who'd offered to pay for a private jet to fly her over or anything.'

'And it's not as if she hasn't seen her daughters in, what? Seven years?'

'Or never met her only grandchild.' Finn, Orla's precious three-year-old son, her miracle of life, currently napping in one of the suite's bedrooms under the watchful gaze of a nurse, had never set eyes on his grandmother.

She met Aislin's stare through the reflection of the mirror and they burst into peals of laughter.

The sisters had long ago learned that the best way to keep the anger and pain of their mother's actions at bay was to laugh and treat it all as one big joke. If they didn't laugh there was a good chance they would never stop crying.

'I suppose you should be grateful she remembered,' Orla pointed out dryly.

'I'm brimming with gratitude.'

She sniggered before confiding, 'I'm dreading meeting Dante's mother.' Orla's conception had been the catalyst for Dante's parents' divorce twenty-seven years ago.

'Don't be. I told you, she has no animosity towards you.'

'But she sounds terrifying.'

'She's hilarious. When Dante told her she was going to be a grandmother the first thing she said was that she didn't want to be known as Nonna.'

'What will she be called?' Another two clasps were hooked in quick succession.

Aislin cackled wickedly. 'Nonna!'

'Is she here yet?' 'Here' being the magnificent luxury hotel nestled on a cliff overlooking the Tyrrhenian Sea that Dante had hired the entirety of for the weekend.

'She's going straight to the cathedral with Giuseppe.' Giuseppe was Dante's latest stepfather, Immacolata's sixth husband. 'Now stop whittling.'

Before Orla could make a cutting retort, there was a knock on the door. A moment later a member of the hotel's staff walked into the suite carrying a huge bouquet of flowers in a vase.

'Compliments of the owner,' he said in careful English.

'How lovely.' Aislin clapped her hands in delight. 'Please, put them on the windowsill and, please, thank Mr Valente for me.'

Valente?

For no reason she could imagine, the hairs on the nape of Orla's neck lifted and her gaze flew to the door that concealed her napping child.

When they were alone again, Aislin met Orla's eyes again in the reflection of the mirror. 'Have you met the owner of the hotel yet?'

Now the hairs on her arms lifted too.

'Should I have?' she asked nonchalantly, even as she ground her bare feet into the soft, thick carpet and ice raced up her spine.

Orla had arrived the day before but Finn had been exhausted from the journey, so they'd dined in the suite together rather than join the other early arrivals for the evening meal. By the time Aislin had joined them, both she and Finn had been fast asleep. Her sister had crawled into the bed with her, just as she'd done throughout their childhood. It had been a bittersweet moment for Orla, waking to find her sister asleep beside her. Her baby sister would never share her bed again.

Aislin shrugged but there was a shrewdness in the reflecting stare that sent the ice already in Orla's spine spreading through her limbs. 'Tonino's one of Dante's ushers—they're old friends. Their fathers were friends too.'

Orla's fingers tightened reflexively. Her chest tightened. The room began to swim around her...

'Ouch!'

Aislin's squeal pulled her sharply back into focus and Orla suddenly became aware that her nails were digging into her sister's back. She whipped her hand away...and pulled the clasp she'd had hold of away with it.

Tonino Valente stood by the huge entrance doors and waited for the last guests to file into the baroque cathedral.

The groom, Dante, was at the altar mopping his brow with a handkerchief.

He could laugh to see his old friend acting like this, but propriety forced him to bite his cheeks and smother it.

Who would have thought Dante Moncada, the biggest player of them all, would be standing at the altar sweating with nerves as he awaited his bride? Out of their gang, which decades before had ridden round Palermo on scooters desperately trying to look cool and impress the girls, Dante had always been the one who'd vowed never to settle down. Tonino had been the only one to assume he would one day marry and yet here he was, the last bachelor of their gang left on the shelf.

He'd almost married once. He'd even gone as far as to book this same cathedral before fate had stepped in in the form of an Irish temptress and turned his life inside out with one locking of eyes.

Strangely, Dante was himself marrying an Irishwoman. Tonino had only met her the once, fleetingly, a stunning redhead who had transformed his old friend into a smitten lovesick fool.

What was it with Irishwomen, he ruminated, that they could turn a Sicilian man's head so completely?

His own Irishwoman… Well, that had been an extremely short romance. But intense. Incredibly intense. And then she'd left without saying goodbye. Not a word. Just packed her bags and left. When he'd called, he'd found himself unable to get through—she'd blocked his number.

Her cruelty in the manner she'd ended things had been breathtaking.

He could hardly believe that four years on he still thought about her.

A commotion outside the entrance had him striding outside to help a young couple struggling to manoeuvre a wheelchair-cum-pushchair that had a small child in it up the cathedral steps.

'You're with the bride?' he asked in Sicilian then repeated in English once they were inside and out of the late-afternoon heat. The ushers had all been warned the bride's nephew had mobility issues. A special place at the front of the cathedral had been set aside for him so he could have an unrestricted view of the ceremony. An usher would be required to wait with the child until the bridal party arrived and his mother, the chief bridesmaid, could take over. Tonino guessed the job had become his.

'We are,' the young woman confirmed proudly, her Irish accent strong. 'I'm Aislin's cousin Carmel, and this is my husband Danny. This young man here is Finn.'

'He's Aislin's nephew?' he clarified, just in case there was another wheelchair-bound small boy coming.

'Yes. Aislin and the others left the hotel right behind us so will be here any minute.'

Figuring he should introduce himself so

as not to scare the child, he got down on his haunches and looked at him.

Dressed in a miniature suit that matched the groom's, the boy couldn't be much older than a toddler. He had a shock of thick black hair and equally dark eyes...

There was something about his eyes that made the words Tonino was about to say stick in his throat.

After a drawn-out beat, he conjured a smile. 'Hello, Finn. I'm Tonino. I'm going to take you to the front of the cathedral to wait for your mummy.'

He was rewarded with a wide smile that displayed a row of tiny white teeth.

Straightening, Tonino took the handles of what was clearly a specially made wheelchair and pushed the child down the wide aisle to his designated space. Finn immediately spotted Dante at the altar and flung his arms out as if reaching for him.

Dante grinned and hurried over to crouch on his haunches before him just as Tonino had done. Finn's skinny arms wrapped around his uncle's neck. 'Carry,' Finn demanded in a strong Irish accent.

'Soon,' Dante promised. 'I need to marry Aunty Aislin first.'

'Then carry?'

'You bet. Now be a good boy and wait for

your mummy. Tonino will look after you until she gets here.' Dante kissed his nephew's cheek and ruffled his hair then made his way back to his place at the altar.

Tonino was used to small children. His brother had two, his sister had just given birth to her third. Mobility issues aside, there was nothing about this child that should capture his attention and yet... There was something about him...something familiar. Something that made his skin prickle and his heart pound.

'How old are you, Finn?' he asked through a throat that had run dry.

The little brow creased before he held three fingers up.

'You're three?' he clarified sceptically. The boy was tiny.

A nod.

'You're almost a man.'

The tiny white teeth flashed at him again.

An audible change amongst the congregation caught their attention. The little boy craned to look around him. 'Mummy!'

The bridal party had arrived.

The beautiful bride made her way down the aisle arm in arm with her proud father, identical beams on their faces. Behind them, holding the long train of the bride's dress, were two adorable little girls walking either side of a slender brunette in a long, ancient-Greek-style dusky rose bridesmaid dress. Her face was turned to the child on her left and so hidden from Tonino's sight.

'Mummy!' Finn called out again, this time loud enough for the whole congregation to hear.

The pounding in Tonino's chest ramped up in speed.

And then he caught full view of the brunette's face and his heart stopped beating altogether.

Orla held on to the train of Aislin's dress as if it were life support. She could do nothing to stop her legs trembling.

Tonino Valente. The name she'd spent three years desperately trying to remember. Aislin had uttered his name and in that instant a light had switched on in Orla's brain. If she hadn't ripped the tiny clasp from Aislin's dress she might very well have fainted, but the panic over ruining the hundred-thousand-euro dress had been equal to the shock of recognition at Tonino's name.

The flurry of activity that had followed, the hunt for the designer, who'd eventually been found in the hotel bar and who'd given Orla more evil eyes during the fixing of the clasp than she'd previously received in her lifetime, the arrival of Sabine's daughters—Orla's fellow bridesmaids—and the arrival of Aislin's father... Suddenly the suite had been crammed with people and she'd been forced to get a grip of herself.

This was the biggest day of her sister's life. Aislin had put her life on hold for three years for Orla and Finn. Orla would never have been able to bear the scars that marked her body inside and out without her sister's steadfast support. More than support. Aislin had raised Finn for the first eighteen months of his life, been the first to realise he wasn't developing as he should, the one there every single day of Orla's rehabilitation.

And now it was Orla's turn to support her sister; her protector, her best friend, her guardian angel made flesh. This was Aislin's day.

Sick dread continued its steady drum as they moved closer to the altar and she had to use all her concentration to keep the train of Aislin's dress stretched out and keep control of the little bridesmaids by her side, both of whom were merrily waving at the packed congregation as if they were royalty. She hardly dared look away from them in case she found the dark brown stare that had haunted her dreams.

Could it really be him?

It had been almost four years. All they'd shared was one night. Or was it two? Or three?

Or more? She wished she could remember but her memory had as many holes in it as a lump of Swiss cheese. Many of the holes had closed with time and the lost memories had returned but everything to do with Tonino and her time in Sicily remained blurry snapshots. She knew they'd met at the hotel she'd checked into during her fruitless attempt to meet her father, but that had been her only concrete remembrance... apart from his face. She remembered that handsome face vividly. Every time she'd pictured it, she'd had to suck in a breath of air to counteract the lance of pain that had accompanied it and blink away tears she'd had no clue from whence they had come.

'Mummy!'

Her son's voice broke through the fog of fear in her head.

Stretching her cheeks into a smile, she finally had a clear view past her sister to the spot at the left of the altar where she'd been promised she and Finn would sit.

The smile froze, half formed.

A tall, dark, utterly gorgeous man sat beside Finn. His black stare was fixed directly on her.

Her stomach plummeted. Thick heat pulsed and swirled through her head, dizzying her.

She had no recollection of Aislin's father handing the bride to the groom, no recollection of the two small bridesmaids leaving her side, no recollection of her feet taking her to her son. All she remembered from taking those steps was the blazing heat that suffused her entire body and the feeling that she could fall into a dead faint from the shock.

The man watching over her son until she could take her place beside him was Tonino. Finn's father.

CHAPTER TWO

THE WEDDING CEREMONY passed Tonino by. He rose and sat when directed, joined in with the hymns, recited the prayers at the appropriate times but it was all noise. He could not switch his attention away from Orla. Or her child.

The child who looked the image of his own childhood photographs.

His eyes flew from mother to child, child to mother, his gaze unable to settle any more than his ragged heartbeats could.

The pounding in his head was too strong for coherent thoughts. He couldn't breathe properly. He'd only been capable of snatching drags of air into his lungs since he'd seen Orla's face.

He'd risen from the seat he'd been saving for her and they'd stepped around each other, eyes locked, like two moons orbiting an invisible sun. For the first time in his thirty-four years he'd been struck speechless.

Her green eyes had been wide. Frightened. Her face had been white.

That was the last time their gazes connected.

Not once throughout the ceremony did Orla look at him. While his stare remained resolutely upon her and her child, her attention, when not taken by her son, stayed on the bride and groom.

Gradually, anger and incredulity rose inside him and pushed out the shock. Coherent thinking returned. His wits sharpened.

He began to see more clearly too. And what he saw proved that, despite having had a child, Orla hadn't changed at all.

She was still beautiful. Slender and elegant. The long, thick dark hair he'd last seen spread over his pillow when he'd kissed her goodbye was coiled into a chic knot on the nape of her neck. The elfin features he'd once thought belonged on the pages of a fairy-tale book had been expertly made-up, smoky eye shadow emphasising the stunning large green eyes he'd once gazed into while buried deep inside her. The long-sleeved dress she wore was far less revealing than usual bridesmaid dresses, the dusky pink silk wrapping around her body to kiss her gentle curves but displaying minimal flesh.

Her beauty had captivated him from the first look.

That first look had been pure chance. A member of his public relations team had found a litany of complaints about one of his Palermo hotels online. Tonino had rearranged his itinerary and headed straight there. The Palermo hotel in question had been part of his uncle's struggling chain until Tonino had stepped in to save it and save his uncle's reputation from the shame of bankruptcy. Where Tonino specialised in converting old castles, monasteries, chateaux and the like into luxury spa and golf resorts for the wealthy, his uncle's hotel chain had been aimed firmly at holidaymakers on a budget.

Tonino had been raised in a wealthy family but his core group of childhood friends had come from diverse economic backgrounds. Gio, the friend Dante had chosen as his best man, came from an exceptionally poor background. In their school days, holidays for Gio's family had been the result of months of overtime, scrimping and saving. The cost of their holiday had been pocket change compared to the sums spent by visitors to Tonino's own hotels but in comparison had cost them far more and had meant a hell of a lot more as a result. He always thought of Gio when inspecting his lower-ranked hotels. Why should guests be forced to accept shoddy service, cold food and an unclean swimming pool just because they were poor? It was this exact same argument he'd had with his hotel manager right before he'd fired him. He'd left the meeting room, furious at the fired manager and furious with himself for allowing the situation to get this far. A solitary woman had been waiting at the unattended reception desk.

That woman had been Orla.

His reaction to her had been like a knockout punch to his guts. He'd never had such an immediate reaction to a woman before and it had been the final clarion call needed to know he couldn't marry Sophia. That reaction had been the unwitting trigger for the rift that still existed between Tonino and his parents. That knockout initial reaction had changed the course of his life.

Orla was thankful for the bossy photographer. He clearly saw himself as an *artiste* and spent ages framing each shot in the cathedral's picturesque grounds. This allowed her to hide in plain sight with her family, safe amid their huge numbers. That she had barely spoken to any of them in the last three years was neither here nor there. She felt no animosity towards them. They simply picked up where they'd left off, catching up on their lives in snatches of conversation.

Snatches of conversation were all she could

manage. Everything inside her had become so tight it was a struggle to get any words out.

One of the small bridesmaids had taken a shine to Finn and stuck to his side, gabbling away to him in her own language. Finn didn't have much in the way of a vocabulary but the rapture on his face only proved that language was inconsequential.

Too scared to look at Tonino, Orla kept her gaze far from him but still felt the heat of his stare upon her. It had been hard enough feeling it every second of the wedding ceremony but outside, his solid form a good head taller than most of the other guests, she felt his attention like a malevolent spectre haunting her. She sensed his loathing, which only added to the cold needles digging into her skin.

What had she done to provoke such animosity?

Deep in her bones she knew the moment opportunity presented itself, he would pounce. She had to be ready for it. She *had* to remember.

Frustration at her Swiss cheese memory made her want to scream.

She'd been waiting for her baby to be born before telling the father. That was something she knew only because Aislin had told her so. Aislin had been unable to tell her the father's name or Orla's reasons for waiting until after the birth to tell him because Orla had never disclosed it to her.

Why was that? Orla never kept secrets from her sister so why would she have kept something of such importance to herself?

There were so many things she'd spent three years trying to understand about her own thoughts and actions during the pregnancy, desperately trying to remember, even undergoing hypnosis to unlock the crucial hidden memories.

The most crucial memory of all, the identity of Finn's father, had now been unlocked but there was still a heap of others to bring to light.

As soon as the photos were done and the bride and groom had ridden off to the hotel on their horse-drawn carriage, Orla latched onto Aislin's friend Sabine and used her as a shield while she wheeled Finn to their waiting car.

She unstrapped him and carefully lifted him into her arms. He was small for his age and light in weight but it wouldn't be long before her still-weak muscles would struggle to carry him any distance. She would carry him for as long as she could physically manage. She'd missed out on so much of his short life, days and nights spent aching to hold her baby, days and nights spent hating the body that had entrapped her in a living hell, fighting with every breath to get herself well enough that she could at least live under the same roof as her child.

Once Finn was secured in his car seat, she hurried to the other side and slid in beside him.

Only when the driver pulled away did she turn her head to look out of the window.

Tonino was staring straight at her, not a flicker of emotion on his handsome face.

Mercifully sat at the top table, Orla watched the seven-course wedding meal unfold around her in the hotel's enormous ballroom decoratively adorned with balloons and glitter. She had been seated on the top table beside Aislin's father, the man who'd been Orla's stepfather from the age of three for the grand total of two years. Aislin had so many of Dennis O'Reilly's characteristics that being in his company was usually a joy. A humble man who'd been treated atrociously by their mother, he'd always treated Orla with great kindness on the occasions she'd seen him after the divorce.

Today though, she couldn't relax long enough to find the usual enjoyment she would have found being next to him.

This was hands down the most luxuriant and glamorous wedding she'd ever attended. The food was the most delicious she'd ever eaten, the wine in her glass the nicest she'd ever sipped;

even the water had a purity to it she'd never tasted before. She could take no pleasure from any of it.

To her misfortune, Tonino had been placed to the left of the top table, facing her. Every time she glanced in his direction, she found his cold stare on her. It never failed to send a shiver up her spine.

Something different raced up her spine whenever she caught sight of the stunningly beautiful blonde woman with eyes like a cat seated to the right of the top table. Orla was certain she wasn't imagining the death stares being thrown by her, which were far more potent than the daggers she'd received from Aislin's wedding-dress designer.

She *knew* this woman. But from where? And why did she want to hide under the table to escape her?

Her torrid thoughts were interrupted when Dennis got to his feet, tapped his glass for attention, and pulled out a sheet of paper.

Much merriment ensued. Even Orla found her lips pulling into an unforced smile to see the Sicilian guests' bemusement. Dennis's accent was so thick and he spoke so quickly they probably struggled to understand him. The Irish contingent understood him perfectly and heckled liberally. Only one brave strapping teenager dared heckle Dante when it was his turn to speak, though, and was rewarded with a slap from his pint-sized mother, which had Sicilians and Irish alike laughing.

After the speeches were done and copious toasts had been made, there was an hour of free time. Many of the guests disappeared to their rooms to change for the evening party. Most of Tonino's table stood too, but the tiny easing in Orla's chest at the fact that he might leave the ballroom tightened again when, eyes locked, he strode towards her.

Fear scratched at her throat. She wasn't ready for this. She needed to make sense of the unfolding memories before the confrontation that had to happen occurred.

Fate stepped in in the form of Dante's glamorous mother, Immacolata, who Aislin had been right in saying held no animosity towards Orla. Immacolata pounced on Tonino when he was barely three feet from the table.

Snatching the opportunity to escape, Orla hurried to her feet and took hold of Finn's wheelchair. *I'm taking him to the suite*, she mouthed to Aislin.

Are you okay? Aislin mouthed back.

She nodded vigorously. 'I need to get his walker.'

Luck shone on her again when a handful of

her cousins' small children bounded over and loudly insisted on accompanying them.

Guarded by an army of children barely out of nappies—the bridesmaids tagged along too—Orla took Finn to their suite.

Leaving Finn's nurse to keep order over the sugar-loaded kids, she stepped out onto the balcony alone. Familiar scents filled her airwaves and, slowly, the vertigo-like feeling that had cloaked her since she'd heard Tonino's name that morning lifted.

She gazed out at the Tyrrhenian Sea darkening under the setting sun. The Sicilian aromas weren't the only things stabbing at her memories.

She craned to her left and squinted, trying to spot the run-down beachside hotel she'd stayed in when she'd met Tonino...

Whether it was seeing Tonino again or being back in Sicily she couldn't say, but the locked-away memories that had eluded her since she'd woken in hospital were slowly taking substance in her mind, but it was all still a jumble.

Sophia!

That was the cat's-eyed, dangerous-looking woman's name. Sophia. She'd confronted Orla...but about what?

Stupid brain, *work*!

A squeal of laughter from the suite shook her from the reforming jumble of memories. The evening reception was about to start. She had to be there.

She got her army of children together and, the nurse carrying Finn's walker, they trooped out of the suite and down the corridor.

Into the lift they all piled. Seconds later they reached the ground floor, the doors opened and the excitable kids burst out like a spray of rubber bullets.

Orla's brief amusement died when she noticed the imposing figure propped against the wall.

Tonino pulled himself away from the wall he'd stood against while waiting for Orla to reappear. All the hotel's stairs and elevators exited at this corridor. She could not escape without him seeing her.

Or her seeing him.

When she appeared, the little colour she had on her milky-white complexion drained away.

Let her feel fearful. Let her take in her surroundings and know there was no escape from him, not here in his own hotel where he had staff posted on every exit into the grounds, ready to notify him should she decide to escape further than her suite.

He stood right in front of her, but it was not his deceitful ex-lover he addressed.

Crouching down, he held out a hand to the child he strongly suspected was his own, and not only because of the uncanny resemblance between them.

Orla had been a virgin. He remembered the flame of colour that had stained her cheeks when she'd told him that and had to fight back the memory snaking through his blood of the first time he'd made love to her.

'Hello, Finn. Are you having a good time?'

Finn nodded vigorously. He strained forwards but the straps of his wheelchair stopped him leaning too far.

'And do you like your suite?'

He was rewarded with a blank stare.

'Your room,' Tonino clarified. 'Do you like your room?'

Another vigorous nod.

'You're sharing it with your mummy?'

A less vigorous nod.

'What about your daddy? Is he sharing it too?' Having checked the room and suite allocation, he already knew the answer to this, but he wanted to see Finn's reaction to the word 'daddy'. Dante had been uncharacteristically evasive on the subject of Finn's parentage when he'd tried to quiz him a short while ago. Tonino understood. Orla was Dante's newfound sister. He had a sister himself. Blood protected blood. It had been Aislin's reaction to his questions that had been the biggest giveaway. She'd reminded him of a cornered rabbit.

The blank stare returned.

A little voice piped up, the Irish brogue strong. 'Finn doesn't have a daddy.'

Tonino raised his head to look at Orla. She was clasping the handles of the wheelchair so tightly her knuckles had whitened.

The expression on her face along with the child's unwitting answer was all the confirmation he needed.

Her green eyes held his, wide and pleading, before she gave a slight shake of her head and mouthed, *Later. Please,* and expertly pushed the wheelchair around him and aimed it towards the ballroom at a speed that would suggest she was being chased by a pack of rabid dogs.

Suddenly feeling in need of a large drink, he let her go.

The ballroom had been transformed into an even glitzier spectacle by the time Orla hurried through its doors. The main lights had dimmed so the only illumination came from the glittering chandeliers. The DJ had started playing music but the dance floor was empty.

The fear gripping her heart tightened when she saw her sister's face.

'Tonino Valente was asking questions about Finn's father,' Aislin whispered when she reached her.

Terrified she was going to cry, Orla blinked frantically.

Sympathy and understanding washed over her sister's face. 'It's him, isn't it?'

All she could do was nod.

'He knows?'

Pulling her lips in tightly, she nodded again. Tonino had taken one look at Finn and recognised him as his own.

'What are you going to do?'

'I don't know.' For three years she'd waited for the memories to return, assuming that, once she had them back, she would enlist her sister's help and set off to find Finn's father. She would have had time to prepare herself.

Never in her wildest dreams had she imagined a scenario like this.

Behind Aislin, Dante approached them.

His presence brought some much-needed sanity to Orla's frazzled nerves.

Whatever happened, she mustn't lose sight that this was their big day. If Aislin so much as suspected the fear in Orla's heart then everything would be ruined. She wouldn't hesitate to cancel the party or the honeymoon.

Flinging her arms around her, Orla held her

sister tightly. 'I need to settle my nerves but I'm going to be fine. I promise. Now stop worrying about me and enjoy your party.'

On cue, the DJ called for the bride and groom to take to the dance floor.

'Go,' Orla urged, kissing Aislin's cheek. She was rewarded with a kiss in return.

While Dante led Aislin onto the dance floor, Orla took Finn out of his wheelchair and put him in his walker, a wonderful device Dante had bought for him that kept him secure and allowed him to use his legs to get himself about. She had to be careful with the amount of time he used it as he tired easily, but she knew he would want to get on the dance floor with the other children.

As soon as he was in it he started bouncing with glee. His 'girlfriend' the bridesmaid shot over to admire him in it.

Orla went with them to the edge of the dance floor with the other guests.

Tears she'd been holding back filled her eyes again to see the love shining between the two people she loved so much. She didn't need to pray for their love to be eternal. Aislin and Dante were made for each other.

As the dance came to an end an arm brushed against hers. Her skin tingled.

A spicy scent filled her nostrils. Her pulses

surged. Her lungs tightened. A memory of pressing her nose into a strong neck and inhaling this scent flashed through her.

'I give them six months.'

She didn't dare look at him. Somehow she managed to croak, 'What?'

'Their marriage. If Aislin has your blood in her veins then it won't be long before her mask slips and Dante realises that beneath the pretty surface lies a black, deceitful heart.' A huge hand closed on her wrist. 'Dance with me.'

She thought her knees were about to collapse beneath her.

'Dance with me or I make a scene. Do you want to be responsible for ruining your brother and sister's special day?'

He gave her no further chance to answer. Before she knew it, Orla was being smoothly manhandled onto the dance floor and pulled against the hulking body of the only man she'd ever been intimate with.

CHAPTER THREE

DANCING WITH ORLA was like dancing with a lump of aged clay. Her arms hung limply by her sides; her movements stiff and resistant.

Taking her hands firmly and placing them on his waist, Tonino dipped his head to whisper into her ear. 'Were you ever going to tell me?'

Somehow she managed to stiffen even further.

A loose strand of her hair brushed against his nose and suddenly he became aware of his sinews tightening and his veins thickening as her scent worked its magic in his senses.

Her magic had once thrilled him. Initially shy, she'd soon revealed herself to be sweet and funny, a woman who wore her intelligence lightly, unaware of her inherent sensual nature until he'd brought it out of her. That was what had made her abrupt disappearance so hard to comprehend. He could have understood if she'd been prickly and had the bitchy streak so many of the women in his world wore like a badge of honour, but she'd been nothing like them.

He could never have imagined she would turn out to be worse than all of them put together.

Disgust that he could still feel such a visceral response to her had him stepping back so their bodies no longer touched.

'Orla, you have hidden my son from me for three years,' he said tightly, loathing that he could feel anything other *than* loathing for this treacherous woman. 'If you want me to keep hold of my temper and not make a scene, I suggest you answer my question. Were you ever going to tell me I have a child?'

A contortion of emotions crashed over her face. Frightened green eyes flickered. Soft, plump lips tightened.

Tonino's self-loathing increased at the vivid remembrance of how good it had felt to have those soft lips crushed against his.

Never had he hated anyone as much as he hated Orla right then. That he could still desire her after everything she'd done stretched credulity to a whole new dimension.

He spun her round in his arms so she faced the socialising guests rather than the DJ. Ignoring the malevolent stares being thrown his way by Sophia and the rest of the Messinas, he said, 'You see the table I was on?'

She gave a tiny nod.

'That is my family. They have spent the day celebrating your brother and sister's marriage. My parents are here, my brother and his family, my brother-in-law and my sister's children... They have all seen Finn, unaware he is their blood.'

Tonino might still feel the residue of anger over the furious arguments that had erupted between him and his parents when he'd ended his engagement to Sophia, but his parents adored their grandchildren. Nothing made them happier than news of another family pregnancy. Babies were celebrated as gifts from God.

'You have deprived them of a grandson, nephew and cousin. You have deprived Finn of his Sicilian family and heritage.'

The anger in Tonino's carefully delivered words chilled Orla's heart. Her brain kept alternating between hot and cold, a vapid mess of confusion, fear and guilt. Being held so close to him only made matters worse. Her heart pounded so hard there was danger it could beat itself out of her constricted chest. Every time she managed to take a breath his spicy scent dived into her airwaves. It shocked and terrified her that her nose seemed to want to bury itself into his neck and breathe his scent in properly, just as it had done all those years ago. It terrified her even more that her hands wanted to wrap fully around his waist and her body strained to press closer against his hard torso.

Being held in his arms had flooded her with more memories.

She remembered taking one look at him and her insides and brain melting into hot goo.

She remembered lying naked in his arms, half awake as the morning sun filtered into the bedroom, and thinking she had never been so happy.

And she remembered learning that everything he'd told her about himself had been a lie.

Orla stared at Tonino's family, her stomach churning violently. These impossibly glamorous, impossibly wealthy, impossibly powerful people were her baby's family. How would they react when they learned of Finn? She knew it was her broken brain's fault that they were not a part of Finn's life but, even as she breathed relief to remember her intentions *had* always been to tell Tonino about their child, she still felt wretched for them. All she'd wanted was to get through the pregnancy, have her baby on Irish soil and then seek legal help before telling him...

Suddenly finding herself meeting Sophia's coldly furious stare, she hastily looked away, straight into Tonino's equally cold and furious stare.

The churning in her stomach increased as she found herself gazing at the handsome face she remembered sighing with pleasure to wake beside.

He was just so...*masculine*. Thick, dark stubble was already breaking out over his chiselled jawline and perfectly complemented the thick, dark hair he wore short at the sides and longer at the top. But, for all his sculptural perfection, it was his eyes she'd always found the most arresting. They were like the darkest melted chocolate. They had made *her* melt.

Their son had his eyes.

Wrenching her stare from Tonino, she found her son bouncing happily in his walker and took a deep breath.

From the moment the pregnancy had been confirmed, her child's welfare had been the focus of her life. When she'd woken from the coma with all memories of the previous six months lost, she'd known, even while everything else had been a blank, that she'd been carrying a child. She would fight to the last breath to keep him safe.

Suddenly desperate to hold Finn in her arms, she dropped her light touch against Tonino's waist and took a step back. 'Please, I don't want a scene but this is not the time or place for this conversation.'

His features darkened. He snatched at her wrist before she could take another step away from him. 'Then let's go somewhere private—this is a conversation we should have had four years ago. You have kept my son in the dark about me for long enough. *Finn doesn't have a daddy?* He damn well does and he deserves to know it.'

'I agree but take a look at him. *Look,*' she insisted when his now blazing eyes stayed locked on hers. 'You must see he's not a well boy. He's looked forward to this day for ages and looked forward to dancing and playing with other children. Let him enjoy the party for another hour and then I'll put him to bed. Give him time to fall asleep and then come to my suite. Please? We can talk then.'

He turned his head to the direction of their son. His chest rose and fell heavily.

Eventually he inclined his head sharply, dropped his loose hold on her wrist and faced her again. 'Two hours, Orla, and then I come to your suite.' He bowed his head to whisper in her ear, 'And if you have thoughts of running away, know I have put measures in place to prevent it. You will never escape from me again.'

* * *

The nurse helped Orla get Finn into his pyjamas and put him to bed before Orla told her to go and join the party for a few hours.

Alone, she stripped off her bridesmaid dress, avoiding the reflection of her bare figure in the mirror. Her scars were itching but she didn't dare apply the topical lotion her doctor had prescribed for it, not when the knock on the suite door could come at any moment. Instead, she dressed hastily, donning a pair of checked trousers and a long-sleeved black top.

When Tonino came she wanted to be ready.

Could she ever be ready for this?

She'd spent three years trying desperately to remember who Finn's father was and unearth the memories of their time together. Now that many of them had popped out of the box they'd been contained in, part of her wished she could shove them back in and nail the lid back down while, contrarily, her search for the still-hidden memories became more frantic.

Much of the time they'd shared together had come back to her, but she still didn't remember what had happened with her father. Her return to Ireland was still a blur too.

When the loud rap on her suite's door finally came, it took more effort than she could believe to drag her legs to it.

Tonino loomed at the threshold looking exactly as she imagined a vampire would in the moments before it swooped to strike its helpless victim.

A vampire should not send her pulses soaring with just one look. That was dangerous by any stretch of the imagination.

Without a word being exchanged, he stepped into the suite and closed the door. Folding his arms across his broad chest, he slowly looked her up and down.

The intensity of his scrutiny sent something thick and warm trickling through her feverish veins. Shaken, Orla hastily sat herself on one of the suite's plush sofas.

She didn't want to look at him but found herself helpless to do anything else. Tonino had such presence, a magnetic energy he carried with him. All the words she'd prepared stuck on her tongue as she gazed into the dark brown eyes of the man who'd swept her off her feet and then broken her heart in the space of ten days. That same broken heart thundered in her chest. Its thuds pounded in her head. Her thoughts, like her words and memories, were a messed-up jumble.

She had no idea how to play this. The man she'd had the time of her life with had been a lie, but he was still Finn's father. He might have all the wealth and power, but he was still Finn's father. When all was said and done, that was the one inescapable fact. Finn deserved to know his father and Tonino deserved to know his son.

After a long period of charged silence, he dragged his fingers through his hair and headed to the minibar. 'I don't know about you but I need a drink. Do you still drink gin?'

Startled that he remembered something so innocuous, she shook her head.

He arched an eyebrow then opened the bar door and pulled out a bottle of red wine.

He took a corkscrew from a drawer and opened the bottle effortlessly. 'Will you have one?'

This time she managed to croak, 'No, thank you.'

Since the accident, Orla had lost all tolerance for alcohol, which was a great shame. Before the pregnancy, she'd loved nothing more than going out with her friends, drinking way too much and dancing until the sun came up. She'd been free. No responsibilities, no pain, no dependency on anyone else. No one dependent on her.

Those days belonged to another woman.

He poured himself a hefty glass, swirled the red liquid, put the rim under his nose then took a sip. It must have pleased his palate for he then took a much larger sip.

Tonino, she suddenly remembered, loved good wine.

When his eyes locked on to hers, a shiver ran down her spine. He looked murderously cold.

'Why don't you sit down?' she suggested quietly.

Tonino, propped against the bar, took another drink as he looked at Orla, dwarfed by the sofa she'd sat herself on, fingers twisting together. She reminded him of a newborn deer that had come face-to-face with its first predator.

'I'm fine where I am,' he answered.

She raised a shoulder and breathed in through her nose. 'Then would you mind not glowering at me?'

That *voice*…

Orla was the only woman who'd turned him on with nothing but her voice. The husky timbre and lyrical brogue were pure alchemy to the senses. It coiled through his veins like the finest of wines and came dangerously close to muffling out her actual words.

'Glowering?' It was an unfamiliar word.

Her lips curled into a brief smile. 'You know—looking like you want to rip my head from my neck. It's making me feel all itchy.'

'You're safe,' he answered sardonically. 'If I

rip your head off I'll never get any answers from you. Enough stalling. Tell me what's wrong with my son and tell me why you have kept him a secret from me for all these years.'

She dipped her head forwards and put her face in her hands. Her fingers dragged through her thick mane of wavy dark hair, which she'd released from its knot. It was every bit as luscious as he remembered and he suddenly experienced the deepest urge to kneel before her and cradle her face in his hands, stroke the soft skin and run his fingers through the thick mane as he'd done so many times before.

When she looked back up to meet his stare, everything inside him clenched.

'Are you sure you won't sit down?' she said softly. 'This could take a while.'

Gritting his teeth tightly, he stared at her. Or glowered, as she called it. He would not allow her soft femininity to weaken him. His height was one of the natural advantages nature had given him, his strength accomplished by his own hard work. If him remaining standing made Orla feel disadvantaged, then great. He saw no reason to put her at ease. On the contrary.

She chewed her bottom lip then sighed. 'I always wanted to tell you.'

He snorted.

'Please, just listen. Finn's condition and the

reason I never told you about him are related. I had a car accident when I was six months pregnant that left my memory shot to pieces. I couldn't tell you about Finn because I'd forgotten who you were.'

Her excuse was so outrageous he tightened his grip on the wine glass to stop himself throwing it against the wall. '*Dio mio*, you have got some nerve, lady. You're claiming you had *amnesia*?'

'Yes. But it's not a claim. It's the truth.'

'And when did your memories return?'

'The ones about you returned today… Well, some of them have…'

'Very convenient,' he mocked, topping up his glass with more wine. 'You've had hours to come up with a convincing excuse and this is the best you can do? Amnesia?'

'I understand it sounds far-fetched but it's the truth. I've spent over three years trying to remember you. All I remembered with any clarity until today was your face. Everything else was hazy images. I knew we'd met here in Sicily but that was a deep-rooted knowledge, like knowing my own name—'

'You expect me to believe this?' he interrupted impatiently.

'It's the truth and it's a provable truth.'

'Really?' he sneered. 'The only thing provable is that you're a liar.'

'I am *not*.'

'You booked into my hotel under a false name.'

Confusion creased her beautiful face. 'What are you talking about?'

'Four years ago you booked into my hotel under the name of Orla McCarthy. Here, you are booked in under the name of Orla O'Reilly.'

Around a month after she'd done her disappearing act, Tonino had drunk too much wine and decided to search her name on the Internet. The few articles he'd found with the name Orla McCarthy in them had not been about her.

Now he understood why Orla had bucked the trend and left no digital footprint. She'd given him a false name.

The woman he'd experienced the deepest connection of his life with, the woman who'd been the unwitting catalyst of the ongoing rift with his family, the woman who'd had no idea of who he was yet had still treated him like a prince...

That woman had lied about her name. She'd kept his child a secret from him.

He couldn't understand why he wasn't fighting an urge to throw her out of the suite window into the sea below but was instead fighting the powerful urge to drag her into his arms and kiss her until he'd drawn all the breath from her lungs.

He couldn't understand how he could look at her deceitful face and feel all his internal organs swelling and compressing his lungs. These were reactions her cruel duplicity should have killed stone dead.

'When I booked into your hotel four years ago I had to hand my passport over so I used my legal name, which is McCarthy,' she explained wearily.

'Then why are you here now as O'Reilly? Was it to throw me off the scent? Did you think I wouldn't recognise you?'

She rubbed her eyes with the palms of her hands. 'I genuinely do not know what you're implying.'

'There is nothing genuine about you,' he said roughly. 'You knew you would see me today. Your brother and I are old friends. You're staying in my hotel. The wedding reception's in my hotel.' He squeezed the back of his neck. 'You took a huge risk in coming here and an even bigger risk bringing Finn with you.'

'I wasn't going to come without him,' she protested hotly. 'Dante never mentioned your name. If he had I would have remembered you sooner, but he didn't. Aislin organised the wedding—she made the booking and checked me in. Aislin has her father's surname because our mother married him. Our mum registered me as Orla O'Reilly when I started school, so I had the same surname as them. Most people know me as Orla O'Reilly.'

'Why didn't you change it legally?'

'That would have been up to my mother and she couldn't be bothered.'

He grimaced and took another large drink of his wine, angry with himself for diverting from the only subject that should matter to him. His son. 'What name have you given Finn?'

'My legal name. McCarthy.'

'Why doesn't he have *my* name?'

'Because I'd forgotten it,' she answered through gritted teeth.

Anger swelled like a cobra poising to strike. 'Then who the hell is named as his father?'

'No one.'

'Now I *know* you're lying,' he snarled. He'd interrupted his lawyer's evening meal to demand he look into the legalities of Irish paternity for him. 'It is illegal not to name the father on an Irish birth certificate.'

She rubbed her eyes again then fixed them on him with a sigh that sounded more exasperated than defeated. 'It isn't if there's a compelling reason.'

'And what compelling reason did you give?' he demanded. 'Your amnesia?'

'Keep your voice down or you'll wake Finn.'

For the first time since he'd entered her suite, a fierceness entered her tone.

He hadn't realised he was shouting.

But, *Dio*, it was taking all his strength not to grab her by the shoulders and shake all the lies out of her until only the truth remained. What kind of a fool did she take him for? Did she seriously think she could play the amnesia line and that he would fall for it? What did she think? That they were players in one of those overacted soap operas his grandmother watched?

Green eyes, wide and wary but unflinching, stayed on him. 'Aislin registered Finn's birth. I'd never told her who the father was so she couldn't name you—'

'You denied my existence?' he roared.

'Keep your voice *down*,' she snapped. 'I'm trying to be sympathetic but you're not making it easy when you keep interrupting me with all your stupid assumptions. Everything I am telling you is provable—you do not have to take my word for it.'

'Good because I will never take you at your word for anything.'

'Good because now you know how I feel about you.'

'What do you mean by that?'

'That you are in no position to act all holier

than thou when you consider all the lies you told me.'

Her assertion was almost as outrageous as her lies about having amnesia. 'You dare try to deflect?'

'Deflection? Okay, then, explain this to me, buster. Why did you tell me you were the hotel manager and not the owner?'

'I never told you anything. You assumed it.' He would not feel guilty about this. He'd intended to tell her the truth about who he was the day she'd run away from Sicily.

Tired eyes blazed with the same anger as coursed through his veins. 'You *let* me assume. I only found out who you really were the day I left Sicily when your fiancée paid me a little visit.'

'What the hell are you talking about?'

'Sophia,' she spat. 'The fiancée you forgot to tell me about. She tracked me down when you were in Tuscany.'

Tonino swirled the wine in his glass and stared hard at her, a rancid feeling forming in his guts. Sophia had taken the ending of their engagement as badly as his parents had taken it. He'd shielded Orla from the fallout. Shielding her had been bliss; the pair of them cocooned in his smallest and plainest apartment, just the two of them, the rest of the world locked out. 'What did she want?'

Orla's skin chilled and a throb pounded in her head to remember the encounter that had broken her heart. 'To tell me you belonged to her and warn me off you. What else?'

He nodded in a thoughtful way, but the blackness of his eyes revealed something very different. 'Let me be clear on this—you are telling me that Sophia Messina, the daughter of one of Sicily's oldest families, tracked you down and warned you off me?'

'That's exactly what happened.'

'She threatened you?'

'Not in words but her meaning was very clear. She knew you'd been cheating on her with me. I can't say I liked the threats she made but I understood where her anger came from. No one likes to be made a fool of.'

He'd made a fool of her and Sophia both. The other woman's threats had been almost as sickening as the proof she'd put before her. So sickening had Orla found it that the minute Sophia had left her room, she'd vomited.

She half feared she could vomit now, from both the memories and the growing ache in her head.

'I ended my engagement with Sophia the day I met you,' he stated flatly. 'If you had stuck around and asked, I would have set you straight. Sophia was playing games with you.'

'You expect me to believe that when all the evidence points otherwise and when we both know you're loose with what truth means?'

He let out a Sicilian word she instinctively knew was a curse but, on a roll, she ignored it.

'You let me believe you were a hotel manager. That was a *lie*. Everything you told me about yourself was a stinking fat lie. Can you blame me for being scared when I learned I was pregnant? All I knew for sure was that you were a liar and a powerful one at that. I refused to tell anyone about you because I was frightened and ashamed and an emotional wreck, and all I could focus on was delivering my baby safely into the world. I was going to tell you about him after he was born but then I had the accident and it changed everything. I couldn't amend Finn's birth certificate after I left hospital because I *couldn't remember your name*.'

When Orla had finished her venomously delivered rebuke, the only sounds in the suite were their ragged breaths. The poison swirling between them was thick enough to taste.

Something else swirled between them too in that small stretch of silence, something that glittered behind Tonino's dark, furious eyes. His jaw was clenched so tightly she could see the angry pulse throbbing on it.

When he finally spoke, every word was elucidated with deliberate slowness. 'Do you know what I think? I think you have backed yourself into a corner and that every word coming from your pretty little mouth is an excuse to justify what you *know* is inexcusable. You hoped to get through the day without me noticing or recognising you and hoped you could get through it without me seeing Finn and recognising my own son. You have cruelly and maliciously kept him from me and, for that, you will pay, and pay by having him cruelly and maliciously kept from *you*.'

CHAPTER FOUR

TONINO'S THREAT RANG loudly in Orla's ears then became a siren when he slammed his glass on the bar and strolled towards the bedroom door.

'What are you doing?' she beseeched, trying her hardest not to panic.

'I'm going to see my son.'

He can't take him from you, she reminded herself. *At this moment, he has no legal rights. Don't panic. Keep calm.*

She took a long breath. 'You're going to storm into a three-year-old boy's room and wake him from his sleep?'

The hateful expression he threw at her wounded as deeply as his threats. He placed his hand on the door knob. 'Do not make me out to be the bad guy in this. I want to see my son.'

'If you go in there you will wake him and you will frighten him.'

His jaw clenched. Seizing this brief moment of indecision, Orla pointed at her phone, which she'd placed on the coffee table. 'You can see him through my phone—look, I'm monitoring him as we speak.'

Now his expression became cynical. 'You watch him sleep?'

'I am tonight. He has epilepsy.'

Lines creased his forehead. A beat passed before he said, '*Epilessia...?* Fits?'

She nodded. She *must* keep calm. Placing a hand to her chest in an attempt to temper her clattering heartbeat, she fought to keep her tone even. 'He has seizures—fits. He's on medication for it, which has helped a lot, but he's had an exciting day and I don't want to risk leaving him unmonitored. Normally the nurse would monitor him but I told her to join the party so we could have some privacy.'

She did not drop her gaze from his cynical, suspicious one and allowed herself only a small breath of relief when he abandoned the door. Then she found she had no breath left to exhale for Tonino had walked over and sat his powerful body beside her.

Her poor clattering heart accelerated into overdrive.

He picked the phone up and studied the live feed on it. After a long pause, he said, 'His... *epilessia*...is it linked to his mobility problems?'

'Yes.' Orla suddenly found her attention distracted by the fingers holding her phone. Those same fingers had once caressed her naked skin...

Heat pumped dizzyingly through her head and she quickly dropped her gaze to the floor only to find Tonino's buffed shoes in her eye-line. He had the biggest feet of any man she'd ever met, and tingles laced her spine and spread to a far more intimate area to suddenly remember another part of his anatomy in proportion to those feet...

'He has cerebral palsy,' she hastily added, keeping her eyes fixed on the carpet so he wouldn't see the flame of colour radiating from her cheeks. How could she feel such things for a man who'd just threatened her with her own child? What was *wrong* with her? 'Lots of children with it have epilepsy.'

A long time passed where all he did was stare at the screen of the phone. Orla used that time to concentrate on breathing. She was exhausted. The day had been long and emotionally draining. Her feelings for Tonino were bound to be all over the place. His emotions were bound to be all over the place too. She must remember that threats made in anger were rarely carried out once tempers had cooled.

'What is cerebral...?'

'Palsy,' she finished for him when he struggled to say it. 'It's a condition caused by brain damage that basically affects the muscles.'

He turned his head to look at her. 'My son has brain damage?'

The flash of distress she witnessed in the dark eyes sent a pang through her heart. Her voice softened. 'Think of it as a brain development issue. Thankfully it doesn't seem that his mental faculties have been affected; I mean, he can speak and make himself understood, but time will tell on that part.' Learning difficulties were common for children with cerebral palsy and something Orla was prepared for. If it turned out that Finn did indeed have them then he would have all the help and support he needed.

'What caused it?'

'The trauma of his birth. He was born three months early—'

A loud incessant knocking on the door interrupted their talk.

'I'd better get that,' she muttered. She hauled herself to her feet and forced her aching legs to take her to the door. She would not let Tonino see how badly she was struggling right then; would not give him any further ammunition to use against her.

She was not in the least surprised to find Aislin there.

Her sister didn't even attempt to make an excuse for abandoning her own wedding reception, looking straight over Orla's shoulder into the suite, her nose wrinkling when she caught sight of Tonino. 'Everything okay in here?'

'Everything's fine,' Orla assured her.

Aislin's eyes narrowed as she eyeballed Tonino again before turning her attention back to her sister and saying loudly, 'You look upset.'

Orla gave a rueful shrug. 'This isn't the easiest conversation I've ever had.'

'I'll bet. Shall I stay?'

The temptation to drag Aislin inside was strong. 'Don't be silly. Go back to your party.'

'I saw Finn's nurse on the dance floor. Are you not coming back down?'

'I'm sorry, Ash, but I'm shattered.' And that was the truth. Orla felt wiped out, physically and emotionally.

'Okay. I'll leave you to it, then.' Her voice rose again. 'I'll keep my phone on me. Call if you need me.'

'I will,' Orla lied. She would rather call their mother for help than ruin Aislin's big day more than she already had.

'I'll see you at breakfast?'

'Definitely.'

'Good.' Then, looking over Orla's shoulder to stare at Tonino one more time, Aislin smiled brightly and said, 'If you harm a hair on my sister's head, I'll kill you. Got it?'

Orla found herself biting back a laugh of hysteria at the shock on Tonino's face.

'Did your sister just threaten me?' he asked when Orla sat back down, this time on an armchair away from him. She was finding it hard enough to concentrate properly without Tonino's scent and body heat addling her brain further.

'Yep.' The only downside with the armchair was that she was forced to look at him. Looking at him definitely addled her brain because it quickly became a struggle to stop herself from looking at him. To stop herself staring at him.

Her eyes yearned to stare. They wanted to soak in every perfect feature on the face she had come so close to believing she could trust with her heart.

'Why would she do that?'

'She's very protective of me. She didn't mean it. She wouldn't actually kill you. Probably just castrate you or something.'

She couldn't hold back the burst of laughter when Tonino reflexively crossed his legs and nor could she stop the laughter turning into tears.

This was all too much. Seeing Tonino again, remembering what they'd shared, how it had ended, his loathing of her, his refusal to listen, his threats… It had been a long, emotional roller coaster of a day and now her body was telling her enough was enough.

Tonino watched the tears fall down Orla's beautiful face with a healthy dose of cynicism. When they'd been lovers he would never have imagined her capable of using feminine wiles to save her own skin. He'd believed her to be too genuine for those kinds of games—for *any* kind of game.

What would she do if he pulled her into his arms for fake comfort? Would she cling to him and produce a few more crocodile tears to soak into his shirt? Would she tilt her head and stare at him with those beguiling eyes, silently pleading with him to kiss her?

And what would *he* do if that course of action became reality?

The burn in his loins gave him the answer.

Every breath he'd taken in this suite had filled his lungs with Orla's scent. He was literally breathing her in, and every atom of his body responded to it.

Furious that his attraction for this duplicitous woman still blazed with such luminescence, he jumped back to his feet and helped himself to more wine.

'I'm sorry,' she whispered. 'I'm not usually a

cry-baby. I'm just finding it difficult to get my head around everything.'

'*You're* finding it difficult?' he sneered. 'How the hell do you think I feel?'

'I can guess.'

'I don't need your fake empathy.' He took a large swallow of wine with a grimace. 'I have discovered that I'm a father and that the mother of my child kept him a secret from me for three years and now I have to deal with threats from my oldest friend's new wife who is also my son's aunt. I didn't even know you *had* a sister.' And neither had he known she was Salvatore Moncada's secret daughter. Until that day, he'd had no idea Dante's recently discovered sister was the lover who'd run away from him.

While outwardly open about who she was, Orla had actually kept her cards very close to her chest. He'd known she'd studied for a degree in zoology—he'd never met anyone who'd studied that subject before so it had stuck in his mind—and that she'd travelled to Sicily in the downtime between ending her graduate job as a veterinary technician and starting her dream job on an Irish conservation project, but it wasn't until she'd disappeared that he'd realised he knew nothing of importance about her.

'Well, I didn't know you had a fiancée so that makes us even,' she fired back.

'I didn't have a fiancée. I ended it with Sophia the day I met you.'

'You *would* say that.' Orla squeezed her eyes shut and rubbed her temples. Her head was now pounding. 'Even if I accepted that you're telling me the truth on this...'

A memory flashed in her mind of sitting on her bed at home, palm flat against her still-flat belly, masochistically searching Tonino's name for the hundredth time and seeing the press report that his engagement to Sophia was over.

How long after she'd returned to Ireland had she read that report? A couple of weeks? The report had made clear that Tonino had ended the engagement.

She could scream. Even if he were speaking the truth about when he ended it, he'd still lied about everything else.

Rubbing her temples even harder, trying not to wince at the pain shooting through her head every time she spoke, she said, 'Whose apartment did you take me to?' She remembered more than waking in his bed now. She remembered the apartment itself.

'Mine.'

'Codswallop. Don't forget my brother is a billionaire like yourself—that was not a billionaire's apartment.'

'It was the first apartment I bought with my

own money when I was twenty. I use it when I want privacy...'

His words rang loud in her head, adding to the growing agony, but pushing at her mind were flashes of what he'd wanted privacy with her for. Those particular memories were still nothing but shimmers yet powerful enough to send a bolt of heat down low in her abdomen.

Once she had craved this man's touch. She'd craved everything about him.

She'd made love to him and created a life with him.

'And as for your brother,' he continued, 'you never told me you were Dante's sister and Salvatore Moncada's daughter. You accuse me of hiding things...' He downed his wine and blew out a long puff of air. 'We are losing focus. We are here, now, for one reason only and that is for my son. He is the only thing that matters.'

If he referred to Finn as 'his son' again she would swing for him. Well, she would if she had the energy, but she could feel it draining from her body. Since the accident Orla had suffered from frequent, often debilitating headaches and this one was turning into a whopper. No doubt stress and exhaustion had conspired together and she wanted Tonino gone before he witnessed it go into full bloom.

When she answered, it took all her remaining strength not to let the pain in her head infect her voice. 'At least we can agree on that. Look, Tonino, can we call it a night? Finn's an early riser and I really need to get some sleep before he wakes up. Hopefully a good night's sleep will put us both in a better frame of mind and we can talk again in the morning about where we go from here.'

For a long time he didn't speak, just stared at her, his jaw clenched, firm lips tightly pursed, a pulse throbbing in his temple. 'Where we go is simple. We tell Finn I am his father and that from now on I am a permanent part of his life.'

'Fine.' At that point she would have agreed to anything to be rid of him. It felt as if she had a big bass drum bashing in her head.

The smile he gave chilled her to the bone. 'And, *dolcezza*, to be clear, if you attempt to leave my hotel with my son before the morning, I will have no hesitation in launching a full custody battle—and it's a battle I will win.'

He let himself out of the suite without a backwards glance.

Tonino took a long breath, arranged his features into what he hoped was a non-threatening expression and then knocked on Orla's door.

He'd done much thinking since leaving her suite, and as the hours had passed the rage inside him had subsided. His behaviour, he recognised, had not been much better than the behaviour he'd accused Orla of, albeit a different kind of abhorrence. For his son's sake, he needed to build bridges.

The door opened just as he raised his knuckles to knock on it a second time.

Orla looked at him as if he were something a stray cat had dragged in. 'What time do you call this?'

He took a beat to soak in the thick dark hair, all tousled and spilling over the thin pink robe wrapped around her slender form, and felt a thickening in his loins as he was taken back four years to their first morning together. They'd taken a shower and afterwards he'd expected her to lock herself in the bathroom to paint her face on as all his previous lovers had done. That she hadn't, that she'd been so comfortable in her skin and so comfortable with him not to feel the need to cover it, had evoked the strangest of feelings in him. Even today he couldn't explain what that feeling was, but he felt it again now as he stared at the pink, plump lips that had fascinated him as much as everything else about her had.

He'd wanted Orla with a needy desperation he'd never felt before or since. He could hardly believe those feelings were still alive in his veins.

Breathing through his mouth to protect his lungs from filling with her scent, Tonino stepped past her into the suite. 'You said Finn's an early riser. He must take after me.' Not that Tonino had had any sleep that night. How could he when he was still trying to comprehend what he'd discovered yesterday?

Forget that every component of his body was heightened for Orla, he was here for one reason only. His son.

'Tonino, it's six thirty.'

'I know.' He looked around the living area of the suite. 'Where is he?'

'His nurse has taken him for a walk around the gardens.'

'This early?'

'He's been awake for over an hour.'

If he'd known that he would have come earlier instead of pacing his own suite impatiently. 'When will he be back?'

'I don't know. It depends if there's anything out there that captures his interest.'

'He likes being outside?' There was so much to discover about his son. A whole three years' worth of living to be discovered, including his birth date.

'He loves it.' Orla padded over to the window and perched herself on the ledge. She cast a quick glance at Tonino before tucking a lock of hair behind her ear and looking out at the early-morning view. 'Unfortunately Ireland's reputation for rain is based on fact—we're not known as the Emerald Isle for nothing—so sunny days are to be cherished.'

'Marry me and he can have sunshine every day.'

She turned her gaze back to him sharply. 'What?'

Tonino sat himself down on an armchair and looked straight at her. 'I have been doing much thinking. I want Finn in my life permanently and the best way I can see to facilitate this is for you to marry me.'

CHAPTER FIVE

ORLA WAS GLAD she was sitting down. There was a good chance she would have fallen over in shock if she'd still been on her feet. 'Are you drunk?'

He didn't look drunk. His hair was damp and even sitting far from him on the windowsill she could smell the heady scent of freshly show-ered Tonino. She was certain that if she'd been placed in a room blindfolded and made to smell his scent, that alone would have been enough to unlock her memories of him.

He hadn't shaved but still looked razor-sharp, dark eyes clear and focused intently on her. The wedding suit he'd worn the day before had been replaced with charcoal chinos and a crisp navy shirt that fitted and enhanced his tall, muscular frame perfectly.

God help her but the man was a bigger sex bomb than her broken brain had remembered.

The four years that had passed since they'd

conceived Finn had not been kind to Orla. The youthful body she'd taken for granted was now marked and scarred, unrecognisable from the body Tonino must remember. She'd never considered herself vain until she'd stood naked before a mirror for the first time after the accident and burst into tears at what had reflected back at her.

Where the time that had passed since Finn's conception had been cruel to her, for Tonino it had been kind. Incredibly kind. Adonis himself would look at Tonino and weep at the unfairness.

It had been Orla's suggestion that the nurse take Finn for a walk. She'd guessed Tonino would turn up early—although not this early—and had wanted to be ready for him. She'd wanted to be showered and dressed and armoured behind make-up. Instead he'd arrived at the same moment she'd been about to step into the bathroom for her shower and found her looking like a scruffy cat lady. She hadn't even brushed her hair. She'd bet good money that he'd done it deliberately to catch her off guard.

She knew she shouldn't care what she looked like in front of him but she did. Right then, her pride was all she had left.

Her shoddy appearance was just one more disadvantage she had against him and she could feel the heat of colour splash her face under the weight of his blatant scrutiny. At least her headache had gone so that was one small mercy.

'Marriage makes excellent sense,' he said with all the confidence of a man used to his words being heeded as if he really were Adonis.

Her stomach twisted violently. She empathised with him, she really did, but did he have to be so entitled and overbearing? And did her heart have to beat so hard and her skin thrum just to share the same air as him?

Speaking through gritted teeth, she said, 'You've known about Finn's existence for five minutes and you've spent most of that time threatening me and calling me a liar and now you want to marry me? Are you sure you're not drunk?'

His eyes didn't so much as flicker. 'I want my son to have my name and to be recognised as his father.'

'You can have that without marriage.'

'My son deserves…'

The turmoil that had been with her all the previous day and had still been there the moment she'd opened her eyes that morning reached its peak. 'Will you stop with all this "my son" malarkey?' she suddenly exploded. 'You know nothing about Finn and for you to keep referring to him as *yours* is doing my head in!'

He straightened, his face twisting with contempt. 'If you hadn't selfishly kept him to yourself, I would already know everything about him. I *am* his father, Orla, and I will damned well be a part of his life and take on all the responsibility being his father entails.'

Her temper evaporated to be replaced by shame at her outburst. Bowing her head, she covered her face with her hands and breathed deeply, in and out, in and out, trying desperately to hold back the threatening tears. Only when she was certain that she could speak without opening the floodgates did she look at him again.

'I'm sorry,' she said quietly. 'I know you're his father. I know you have every right to be a part of his life but it's really hard to listen to all your threats and demands when you have no idea what our lives have been like and the struggles we've had to deal with. You can't just snap your fingers and expect me to roll over and go with it. You need to earn your right to be Finn's father.'

Just as she'd had to earn the right to be Finn's mother.

When Orla had finally been allowed home from the rehabilitation centre, Finn had been eighteen months old and, although too young to understand the concept of parenthood, he'd regarded Aislin as his mother. She would never admit it to Aislin or anyone but seeing her own child naturally gravitate to her sister had been unbearable. It had taken a good year before Finn had turned to Orla when he needed help or comfort.

Tonino's eyes narrowed. The weight of his scrutiny increased but she detected a softening in his stance. 'Then stop fighting me and do what's best for Finn.'

'That's all I've ever done.'

'Then *marry* me.'

Her heart beating fast, Orla found herself scrutinising Tonino with the same intensity he scrutinised her, trying hard to look past the breathtakingly gorgeous features for what was going on in his head. Unfortunately, the mind-reading powers she'd always hoped to one day achieve were as elusive as ever. 'Marriage is not the answer. An unhappy marriage does nothing but produce unhappy children. Finn's a happy child who's suffered enough disruption in his life.'

'There is no reason we could not be happy.' Eyes remaining fixed on her, he reclined back in his seat. 'We were good together once.'

'We were together for barely ten days.' She would not cause another argument by pointing out that in that time he'd actively let her believe a lie. 'We don't know each other.'

'We know the most important thing.'

'Which is?'

'Our compatibility.'

'Sorry?'

'You and me…' He hooked an ankle on a muscular thigh. Something glimmered in his eyes that sent Orla's pulses surging. His voice lowered to an appreciative murmur. 'I remember us as being extremely compatible.'

Something deep inside her heated and throbbed with such force that whatever she'd been about to say stuck on her tongue. Gazing into his eyes was like looking into a chocolate pool swirling with brilliance, and the tight pulsations heating her core spread through her veins and danced onto her skin, every nerve ending in her body stirring, every atom screaming loudly its agreement at his words.

Suddenly fearful of being hypnotised by the whirling depths, Orla wrenched her gaze from him and stared back out of the window, trying her hardest to breathe normally.

She'd prepared herself for more threats and arguments. She had not been prepared for a proposal or caressing words. Given the sticky turmoil raging through her, she thought she preferred the threats and arguments.

Even with her back turned from him, she could feel the heat of his stare penetrating her skin.

Folding her arms across her chest, she rubbed her feeble biceps and closed her eyes.

She remembered waking in Tonino's arms the morning after their first night together, dazed but replete. She remembered the sensation that had flooded her veins and heated her skin at his touch.

But the actual memories of them being intimate together remained locked away. She hoped they never returned. She didn't think she could bear to remember how she had given herself to a man who'd only been using her for his own fun.

Dragging more air into her lungs, she cleared her throat. 'I don't want to marry you, period. It would be a disaster.'

Tonino had known getting Orla's agreement for marriage would be a long shot but once the idea had come to him, he'd recognised it as the answer to all their problems. Marriage would solve everything in a neat, orderly fashion. How could he be an effective father if he lived in a different country from his child?

He would have to work on her and make her see that it would be in Finn's best interest for them all to live under the same roof. Given a little time to dismantle the barriers between them, Orla would come around to his way of thinking. The chemistry that had drawn them together four years ago still burned. He felt its scorch with every word and look exchanged between them. And she felt it too. Every time she tucked a strand of her hair behind her ears he was reminded of all the times she'd done that before and all the other little gestures he recognised as uniquely Orla.

She'd been a breath of fresh air in a world he'd never recognised as cynical until she'd entered it and liberated him. For ten magnificent days he had lived for the moment with the first woman he'd been intimate with who had no idea who he really was. Her every response had been organic. She'd been a virgin but making love to her for the first time…it had felt as if it were his first time too.

Their chemistry was the one thing he didn't need a lie detector for. The urge to touch her breathed through his skin and it took all his strength to keep his focus on the job at hand.

'If you won't marry me then I will come to Ireland with you and have my name added to Finn's birth certificate.' He would not accept anything less than being a true father to his son.

Her body immediately struck a defensive pose. 'That can wait.'

'No, *dolcezza*, it cannot.' Getting to his feet, he joined her at the window. She must have sensed his closeness for her back stiffened and she tucked a loose strand of hair behind her ear.

How many nights had he dreamt of that simple non-seductive gesture?

Orla was the only lover whose scent he could remember simply by closing his eyes. Close his eyes and he could remember the feel of her skin beneath his fingers.

Close his eyes and he could remember the bewilderment to find her gone.

He would close his eyes no more. With Orla, he needed to keep his eyes open and his wits sharpened. Whatever happened from this moment, he would never let her disappear again.

'I understand why I've not been named on it but it has to be done.' He couldn't force her to marry him—more was the pity—but he would do whatever was necessary to close off her options to flee.

Her head turned sharply to face him again. Tonino hadn't realised quite how close to her he'd positioned himself until he saw the sprinkling of freckles across her pretty nose.

'You understand…?' She swallowed. 'You believe me?'

'I spoke to Dante after I left you last night,' he admitted. 'He confirmed your story about the accident and your memory problems.'

Dante's confirmation had left him with a myriad emotions. There had been definite relief—Tonino's instincts all those years ago that Orla was of a different mould from the unscrupulous, duplicitous bitches who lived in his world had not been as off the mark as he'd come to believe—but there had been something else there too, something that had made him feel as if acid had been poured into his guts.

Orla's chest rose sharply then loosened slowly. She pressed her head against the window with a sigh. 'I suppose it's understandable you wouldn't take my word on it.'

'It doesn't change how I feel about you not telling me about the pregnancy,' he warned roughly. He doubted he would ever forgive her for that. 'However, I feel it is in Finn's best interest that I put that issue behind me.'

She gave a short bark of shaky laughter. 'Your magnanimity does you much justice.'

Eyeing her carefully, he rested his hands on the windowsill either side of her thighs, effectively trapping her. 'Are you being funny?'

Fresh colour heightened her cheeks. 'I'm wondering where the proof is that you ended your engagement to Sophia before you took me to bed.'

'I am not a cheat. I have never been unfaithful.'

'I'm supposed to take your word on this?'

'*Sì*. In my world, honour is everything. A man who cannot be taken at his word is no man at all.'

'Now you're being the funny one. Seriously?

A man of your word? When you let me believe you were a humble hotel manager rather than a gazillionaire hotel owner?'

'I never lied to you, Orla. Not in words.'

'Well, that makes everything all right, then!' She smiled brightly but her breaths had shallowed. He moved his face closer to hear her next words. 'You didn't lie to me with words. Grand. You're only prepared to believe me about my amnesia because Dante's backed me up, but I'm supposed to take you at your word on everything simply because you say so. Can you not see why that makes me uncomfortable having you named as Finn's father on his birth certificate?'

A man could drown in the emerald-green pool swirling before him. Orla's robe had parted at her waist, exposing her smooth legs. His blood thickened to see her thighs covered only by a pair of pyjama shorts.

'All I want is to be a father to him.' *Dio*, his voice was hardly above a whisper either. 'Having legal recognition is important to me. I don't want to be forced into taking legal action to get it.'

She swallowed a number of times then croaked, 'That sounds like a threat.'

He clenched his tingling fingers into fists. If he extended either thumb he would be touching those delectable thighs. They were as close as they'd been on the dance floor and yet not a single part of their bodies touched.

Now he was the one to swallow, ridding himself of the moisture that had filled his mouth. 'A threat I have no wish to act on.'

Last night, when he'd been full of anger, all he could think about were his rights and the fact that she had so cruelly kept him from his son. While his anger was still there—her insistence that she'd intended to tell him about the birth after the fact was something he doubted he'd ever believe—he could not escape the conclusion that she was correct that he didn't know his son. And his son didn't know him. Tonino and his mother's relationship might be strained these days but as a child he'd worshipped the ground she'd walked on. To have been ripped from her arms would have destroyed him.

'What do you intend to do with the legal recognition?' she whispered.

His face inched closer to hers. 'Be his father. Orla... I'm not going to launch a custody battle for him. All I want is to be involved.'

Her breaths quickened. 'You're not going to fight me?'

'Our trust issues are a two-way thing we both need to work on but I give you my word that, provided you play fair with me, I will not take Finn away from you.'

'That's still a threat. What does play fair even mean?'

Their faces had got so close he could smell the faint mintiness of her toothpaste.

'That you accept me as his father.'

A glazed quality washed over her eyes. Her face tilted, her voice dropping to a murmur. 'I do accept you as his father.'

'Then let us start again.' His lips buzzed and the tingles on his skin deepened as their mouths drew closer still. 'Put the past behind us for Finn's sake and look to the future...'

Right at the moment their lips brushed together, the door to Orla's suite opened and the nurse pushed Finn in.

'Have you not had your shower...? Oh!'

A bullet ricocheting through the suite could not have parted them more effectively.

Cheeks the colour of beetroot, Orla jumped off the windowsill and hurried to Finn, frantically tucking strands of hair behind both ears. 'Could you do me a favour, please, Rachel, and leave us alone for ten minutes?'

The nurse looked knowingly at Tonino. 'Sure.'

The two Irishwomen's conversation followed by the nurse's abrupt departure from the suite were mere noise in Tonino's head. The desire that had come so close to taking control of him had reversed as he stared at the tiny boy strapped in his wheelchair. Unlike the curious nurse, his innocence meant he had no idea his arrival had interrupted anything.

Orla knelt in front of him and carefully lifted him out. She carried him over to the sofa and placed him on her lap. 'Finn, do you remember me telling you that you had a daddy but that mummy lost him?'

Tonino gave her credit for infusing strength into her voice.

The little head nodded.

'And do you remember me telling you that one day we would find him?'

She'd told him *that*...?

Finn nodded again.

'Well... I've found him.'

The dark brown eyes that were so like his own found his.

Tonino held his breath.

'Finn,' Orla continued. 'This man... Tonino... is your daddy.'

There was a long moment of silence where father and son did nothing but stare at each other. Finn's expression was one of frank curiosity.

Tonino waited with bated breath for his son to speak, waited for the little arms to open up and demand a carry as he'd done for his uncle in the cathedral.

He should have known better. Instead of the

grand reunion he'd spent the night imagining, his son looked back at his mother and said, 'Play blocks now?'

CHAPTER SIX

ORLA HAD NO idea how she'd allowed herself to be steamrollered into flying back to Ireland with Tonino on his private jet. The only fleeting satisfaction she'd found that day had been when she'd entered the jet's opulent cabin and stared into his eyes to airily say, 'Oh, it's just like Dante's plane.'

Saying that had been a sharp but welcome reminder that Tonino might come from an immensely powerful and wealthy family, but that her brother was also immensely rich and powerful. It was a reminder to herself as well as Tonino.

Having a brother was such a new aspect of her life that all too often she forgot that she had him in her corner as much as she had Aislin.

Four years ago, when she'd learned she was pregnant, Dante hadn't known of Orla's existence. She could never have turned to him for help back then. Now, if Tonino did try to pull a fast one and launch a custody battle, she wouldn't have to face it alone or without the means to fight back legally and financially.

Even if she didn't have Dante, she felt differently now than she had four years ago. Back then, she'd been a frightened wreck. If the accident had done nothing else, it had toughened her up.

She had a feeling she would need every ounce of her newfound strength to keep Tonino at arm's length.

They had been moments from kissing.

Kissing!

Her lips still tingled in anticipation of the kiss that had never come. Tonino had caught her in a moment of weakness, she told herself stubbornly. It had been early. Her headache had gone but she hadn't had nearly as much sleep as she needed, leaving her tired, which in itself had weakened her.

That her insides still felt like melted goo could also be explained. She didn't know how to explain it but there must be a rational reason for it somewhere.

As Finn and his nurse were flying home with them, conversation between Orla and Tonino was mercifully limited to pleasantries. Conversation between Tonino and the nurse was a different matter. While Orla read Finn a story,

Tonino quietly peppered Rachel with questions about Finn's condition. There was no godly reason why this should irk Orla so much, but it did. Watching the nurse flick her hair as she answered him irked her even more. When Rachel giggled at a comment Tonino made, Orla tightened her grip on the book to prevent herself from throwing it at the pair of them.

Her silent irritation continued for the duration of the flight. Only when they were back on Irish soil and she breathed the familiar air did she manage to regain some of her usual calm.

She was on home territory now. This was her turf and the drive to her home in Dublin was short.

'Thanks for the lift,' she said with as much politeness as she could muster when his driver pulled up. 'What time shall I expect you in the morning?'

He arched a brow. 'Are you not going to invite me in?'

Oh, how badly she wanted to give him a blunt, 'No,' but knew how ungracious that would seem. She tried to put herself in his shoes. She would want to see the home her child lived in if she were wearing them.

'If I must,' she answered, immediately feeling horrible for her churlish response. The horrible feeling lasted less than a second for Rachel visibly brightened.

'You can stay for a coffee,' Orla added, then immediately panicked as she thought of the jar of instant that had moved to Dublin with her from Kerry and had to be at least a year old.

'This is a nice house,' Tonino commented when he walked into the spacious entrance room. Set in a pretty, quiet, tree-lined street, Orla's home was airy and open-plan, cluttered with toys and books but nonetheless clean. It had a homely feeling he warmed to immediately.

'Thank you,' she muttered.

Crouching down to Finn's level, he touched the tiny hand lightly. 'How would you like to show me your room?'

Finn immediately looked to his mother for guidance. She gave a short but reassuring nod. 'You'll have to carry him—he can't do stairs, I'm afraid. His room's the first on the left.'

'I'll come with you,' the nurse offered.

'I'm sure Finn and I can manage,' he rebuffed pleasantly. His curiosity about the specifics of his son's condition had driven him to ask the nurse in detail about it, which he felt certain had annoyed Orla and contributed to the foul mood she'd fallen into on the flight over. For his part, Tonino felt liberated. Leaving Sicily with his child and future wife—he had no doubt that Orla would come round to his way of thinking on marriage—had lifted his spirits immeasurably.

Tonino unstrapped his son and gently lifted him into his arms. He didn't think he had ever held anything so precious and fragile and his heart bloomed to feel the tiny beating heart pressed against his chest. It bloomed even more when a skinny arm hooked around his neck.

Dark brown eyes that were a replica of his own stared at him solemnly. Tonino stared back, suddenly finding himself dumbstruck at the powerful emotions crashing through him.

Before he took the first stair, he looked at Orla and felt another crash of emotion punch through him.

Taking a deep breath, he carried his son upstairs and entered his bedroom.

It took a few moments before he could take another breath. Finn's bedroom was everything a child's room should be, with its dinosaur curtains, walls covered in dinosaur stickers and ceiling covered in glow-in-the-dark stars. A vast array of stuffed toys was crammed on shelves and in boxes, along with boxes of puzzles and games, boxes of building blocks, books...

But there was no escaping the bed with its bars, there to prevent Finn from rolling out, and no escaping the unobtrusive but recognisable cameras there to monitor him while he slept and no escaping the medical equipment Tonino would have to become familiar with.

There was no escaping that this was a room for a child with disabilities. His child. And, as Tonino took stock of it all, he made a vow to himself that he would do everything in his power to make his son's life as comfortable and as happy as he could.

For the second time in a day Orla had no idea how she'd come to allow Tonino to steamroller her into something, this time finishing the day together eating a Chinese takeaway. Indeed, at one point she'd thought she'd got rid of him— he'd taken one sip of his coffee, wrinkled his nose and then excused himself, saying he would be back. When he hadn't returned an hour later, she'd thought he'd checked into wherever he was staying and decided to stay put.

He'd returned while she was clearing up the mess made while feeding Finn his dinner, carrying a large box, which was revealed to be a coffee machine.

'Where did you get that from?' she'd asked in astonishment. 'It's Sunday. All the shops are closed.'

He'd had the audacity to wink at her before disappearing again, returning an hour later with the takeaway and a bottle of wine. 'I thought you must be hungry too,' he'd explained while making himself at home turning the oven on. 'I saw you only cooked for Finn.'

'I've not had a chance to go shopping,' she'd replied defensively while turning off the grill and switching the actual oven on.

A memory of the two of them sharing a Chinese takeaway in his Palermo apartment had hit her. For some unfathomable reason, tears had blurred her vision.

While their food had kept warm in the oven, he'd helped her give Finn a bath and put him to bed. Having him there in the close confinement of the bathroom then the confinement of Finn's bedroom had put her on edge. As hard as she'd tried only to concentrate on her son, she was acutely aware of every movement Tonino made.

It was only the shock of being in his orbit again and the shock of how close they'd come to kissing making her feel so edgy around him. That would lessen as she became accustomed to his presence in their lives. Sooner or later the tightness in her chest would lessen too and her heartbeat would find its natural rhythm when with him, rather than the erratic tempo it adopted every time she caught his eye or captured a whiff of his spicy cologne. He'd clearly meant what he'd said early that morning about them starting over. He'd spoken to her with only courtesy since. If he still felt anger towards her, he hid it well.

And now they were sitting at her dining table, Tonino clearly so ravenous he didn't care that their food had lost much of its moisture, comfortably drinking his way through the wine while she stuck to water. Orla ate as much as she could manage but it was hard to swallow when her insides were so cramped, hard to work her fork from her hand to her mouth while fighting her gaze from staring at the hunk of a man devouring his food opposite her.

It was the first time they'd been alone since Finn had returned from his walk nearly thirteen hours ago. Since they'd nearly kissed. Without Finn or his nurse's physical presence to distract her, Orla found her awareness of Tonino becoming more than a distraction, throwing her back four years when she'd spent ten days with her entire being consumed by this one man.

'Do you feel better now?' he asked after he'd demolished the leftovers.

'What do you mean?'

He shrugged nonchalantly. 'Only that if looks could kill, the looks you were giving me on the plane over would have struck me dead.'

She had the grace to blush. Not looking at him, she muttered, 'I just wanted to get home.'

He nodded musingly. 'Of course. You were missing your home.'

'Exactly.'

'Have you lived here long?'

'Four months.' Orla, mortified that he'd picked up on her earlier bad mood, mustered something she hoped resembled a smile.

'Dante bought it for you?'

'Aislin bought it.' She wasn't about to explain that the money to purchase it had come via Dante paying her sister a million euros to pretend to be his fiancée for a weekend. Of course, Aislin and Dante had fallen in love over that weekend for real, but the lead-up to their falling in love was a private matter between the two of them. Having been the subject of gossip for the entirety of her life, it was not something Orla ever indulged in. 'Dante paid for it to be made Finn-friendly.'

She finished her water and tried not to stare longingly at the remaining wine in the bottle. Alcohol, she was sure, would help her relax. Or, as was more likely, send her to sleep.

Relaxing in Tonino's company was something that was going to take time. A lot of time.

Now that most of the memories of their time together had returned, she found herself replaying it. Much of it felt as vivid as if it had happened only days ago. She'd been relaxed with him then. She'd found an ease in his company she had never felt with anyone other than Aislin before. It had been as if a stranger she'd known for ever had walked into her life. A stranger who'd made her bones melt with nothing but a look.

It horrified her to find her bones still melted for him. Every time he reached for his glass and his muscles flexed beneath his shirt the baser part of her melted too. Every time she caught his eye her erratically thrumming heart would jolt. Her lips still tingled for the kiss that had never come.

'You and Dante have only got to know each other recently, is that correct?' he asked.

Lord help her but his voice melted her too.

She nodded. 'I always knew about him, but he knew nothing of me. He had no idea he had a sister.'

'Why didn't you find him four years ago?'

'I couldn't go up to a stranger and say, *Hello, I'm your long-lost sister*, could I? It wouldn't have been fair.'

He pulled a rueful face. 'I suppose. So, tell me, was your real reason for being in Sicily to find your father?'

She gave another nod.

'You'd never met him before?'

'I wasn't allowed.'

'Why not?'

She shrugged. 'I was his dirty little secret.'

He winced at her descriptor. 'What changed? What spurred you into seeking him?'

'I became an adult.' She smiled wryly. 'For the first time ever, I had a couple of weeks ahead of me with nothing to do. I woke up one morning and thought to myself that it's now or never.'

'Did you meet him?'

'No. He was abroad when I visited on my first day there. I tried again when you went to Tuscany but I don't remember what happened.'

'So you might have met him?'

She shook her head. 'Aislin always told me I didn't.' She took a deep breath. 'I know it in my heart too. Every time I've thought of him since I've wanted to cry.'

Tonino stared at the downcast face with the lips pulled tightly together and his heart twisted. 'Why didn't you share this with me at the time? I could have helped you. My father and your father were old friends.'

'How was I supposed to know that? You never told me who you really were.' Her rebuke, although politely delivered, hit the mark.

'We were lovers, Orla. You should have told me your real reason for being in my country.'

His mention of them having been lovers sent

colour careering over her neck and cheeks. 'Yes, well, you should have told me you actually owned the hotel rather than just managing it but there you are.'

'There we are.' He winced and mock saluted his agreement, admiring her quick, tart retort. The Orla sitting in front of him had a much sharper tongue than the Orla he remembered. 'Two people who kept things close to their chests while still getting naked together.'

'Don't go there,' she warned. The colour now flamed so brightly he could warm his hands on her face.

'If we hadn't gone there we would never have created Finn together.' He downed the last of his wine and grinned.

She smiled sweetly, then, in a perfectly pitched saccharine voice, said, 'And on that happy note, it's time for you to leave.'

'Are you kicking me out?'

'There's no food left and it's late.'

'Are you not worried I won't have anywhere to stay?'

'No. And you're not staying here, if that's what you're trying to wrangle.'

'I wouldn't dream of it. But, please, let your mind rest easy—I have a place to stay.'

'Good. Best you get going to it.'

'Without an after-dinner coffee?'

'Caffeine is the last thing I need.'

'In that case I shall return early in the morning for it.'

'If you turn up as early as you did this morning, the only thing you'll get is a long wait on the doorstep.'

He got to his feet and gave another mock salute. 'Until the morning.'

'Are you still here?'

Grinning, Tonino let himself out. He'd reached his car when he heard the front door lock behind him.

'You are possibly the most infuriating man in the world,' Orla snapped when she opened the front door the next morning.

Tonino looked at his watch and gave an expression of such innocence that she had to bite her cheeks not to laugh out loud. 'You told me not to come as early as I did yesterday.'

'So you come half an hour later? Seriously? It's seven o'clock.'

'And you're up and dressed and looking beautiful.' She looked as fresh and as beautiful as the clear blue skies covering Dublin that morning. Dressed in a knee-length leaf-green jersey dress, her hair loose around her shoulders, her pretty green eyes enhanced with a touch of mascara, a brush of colour over the high cheek-bones. Fresh, beautiful and damned irresistible.

One day soon, he vowed, Orla would open a door to him with a smile and greet him with a kiss rather than a scolding.

Late into the night he'd lain in his bed thinking back over their time together. The more he'd remembered, the more he'd come to understand why the few affairs he'd had since she'd disappeared had fizzled out with barely a whimper. Their affair had hung over him. It had shadowed him doggedly. Seducing Orla into marrying him would allow him to put the shadows to bed in more ways than one. He would have her in his bed and his child permanently in his life. The fact he would never be able to trust her was irrelevant. He didn't need to trust her. He just needed to marry her, the final step that would prevent her ever disappearing from his life with his son again.

Finn was in his high chair at the dining table. He greeted Tonino with a smile and a wave.

'I was just feeding Finn his breakfast. Why don't you make yourself a coffee while we finish up?' Orla strove to keep her tone polite but she could have cheerfully strangled Tonino. She wished she could say it was some sixth sense that he would turn up stupidly early again that had had her awake before Finn but it hadn't been. It had been the dream of them, in bed together, that she'd wrenched herself out of that had accomplished that feat. She'd sat straight upright, heart pounding, burning and throbbing on the inside, not knowing if the dream had been a replay of something real or just her subconscious imagination, and dived straight into the shower to wash the burning feeling away.

She'd cleaned her skin, but her insides...

Mush. Her insides had been a hot, sticky mush the water couldn't touch. They were still mush.

Her hands were shaking. She could barely hold the spoon to feed Finn.

'Coffee?' Tonino's deep voice reverberated in her ear.

'No. Thank you. Did you want something to eat?' She ground her toes into the floor in a futile effort to stop her right knee shaking too. 'There's bread and cereal in the cupboard.'

Dark brown eyes met hers. 'I had something before I left the hotel.'

'Where are you staying?'

'At Bally House.'

'The hotel?'

'*Sì.*'

'You lucky thing.'

'You have been there?'

'I wish,' she said reverently. Bally House

Hotel was once a medieval village with its own church and flour mill. A huge renovation undertaken a few years ago had transformed it into Ireland's premier hotel, the destination of choice for A-list stars to marry in. 'I tried to talk Aislin into getting married there but she wasn't having any of it—she was set on marrying in Sicily.'

'We can marry there.'

'We're not getting married.'

'I am confident that one day soon you will come around to my way of thinking, *dolcezza*.'

'And I am confident that you are full of misplaced ego. I will not marry you, end of subject.'

Mercifully, the nurse descended the stairs, cutting the conversation short.

Less mercifully, the look in Tonino's eyes told her this was a subject he had no intention of dropping.

CHAPTER SEVEN

'ARE YOU OKAY?'

Ever since they'd left the government offices where they'd officially added Tonino's name as father on Finn's birth certificate, Orla had lapsed into silence. Her head was turned from him, her body pressed against the door as if she were preparing to make an escape the moment the car came to a stop.

'I'm fine.' Her tone suggested she was far from fine.

'You do know this is for the best?'

She twisted her head to meet his stare and sighed. 'Yes. I do know that. Whether you believe me or not, I always intended to tell you about Finn. Always.'

Tonino looked at his son—now his *legal* son—fast asleep in his car seat.

He wanted to believe her. For their son's sake. But he couldn't escape the one verifiable fact that she'd made the deliberate choice to keep him in the dark about the pregnancy before the accident. Blaming Sophia's deliberate sabotage was too easy—and he did believe that Sophia had confronted her; it was exactly the kind of thing the poisonous bitch would do— Orla should have told him about the pregnancy whether she believed he was engaged or not. Instead she had chosen to swallow Sophia's lies and deprive him of the wonder of experiencing the pregnancy with her, which in turn had led to depriving him of over the first three years of his son's life. Tonino, as his parents would testify, had never been one for forgiving or forgetting.

'Can I ask you something?' she said after a long period of time had passed when he'd left her assertion unacknowledged.

He loosened his tense shoulders and inclined his head. 'Anything.'

'Last night you said our fathers were old friends. Did you know Salvatore well?'

'Well enough. Why do you ask?'

'I know so little about him. I don't like to ask Dante because I can see it makes him uncomfortable. I think he feels guilty that they had such a great relationship while I was this dirty little secret.'

He could understand why she felt like that. No one had known of Salvatore Moncada's secret love child, not even Tonino's own father, who had been Salvatore's closest friend.

He wondered how his father would react when he learned Salvatore's illegitimate daughter was the mother of his grandchild. Probably with open arms. His mother too. There hadn't been a single conversation between Tonino and his parents in recent years where the subject of him settling down and having babies hadn't come up, the implication being he needed to find a suitable replacement for the fiancée he'd so callously thrown away. In his parents' eyes, Sophia had been perfect. Beautiful and rich and from a good Sicilian family. Their engagement had been celebrated in the same way the British celebrated a royal engagement. Their fury at him ending it had been off the charts. They'd taken it personally. They'd accused him of disrespecting the family name and destroying the decades-long friendship with the Messinas. There had been threats. At one point he'd thought his mother was going to slap his face.

That marriage to Sophia would have seen Tonino spend his life in misery hadn't concerned either of them.

With a sigh, he tried to think positively of his parents. He'd had the security of their unconditional love for the first thirty years of his life whereas Orla had never met her father and as for her mother...where was she? She'd missed Aislin's wedding. Orla rarely spoke of her. She might as well not exist.

'Your father was a man of many contradictions,' he told her heavily.

'In what way?'

He thought of the best way to put it before saying, 'He was a womaniser and a gambler. But he was also a great raconteur. He could tell the most boring story and make it funny. He was not a man anyone would trust to lend money to if they wanted to get it back and definitely not someone any man could trust to leave his wife alone in a room with.'

Her eyes widened with alarm. 'He was a sex pest?'

'No. Women loved him. Some loved him a little too much. He broke many hearts.'

Her lips tightened as she considered this before giving a decisive nod. 'He didn't break my mother's heart.'

'Then she was clever enough not to involve her heart.'

'But not clever enough not to get herself pregnant by a married man.' She closed her eyes and rested her head against the leather upholstery. 'Still, who am I to judge her for it? I did exactly the same thing.'

'I wasn't married, and neither was I engaged,'

he told her firmly. 'And I shouldn't have to tell you that you didn't get pregnant on your own. We were both there.'

She twisted her head again to look back at him. The faintest trace of colour flared on her cheeks as she asked, 'Didn't we use protection?'

'Of course we did.'

'Then how did I end up pregnant?'

'We weren't always as careful as we should have been...' He thought of the few times they'd come together in their sleep, Tonino already deep inside her before waking fully and realising he hadn't put a condom on. He'd withdrawn to sheath himself, knowing even then what a huge risk they'd taken. It was a risk he had never taken before or since, half asleep or otherwise.

Gazing into her confused green eyes, he felt the burn in his loins that had been such a huge part of him in their time together afresh and found himself leaning closer to her, close enough that the soft scent of her perfume coiled into his aroused senses. 'Do you not remember?'

The colour on her cheeks became a burn to match what was happening in his loins. 'No.'

'But you remember us?'

'I remember most of it, but I don't remember...' she swallowed '...the actual act.'

He leaned a little closer still and lowered his voice. 'There was more than one act.'

Her jaw clenched while her eyes darkened and her voice lowered to match his. 'I don't remember anything we did in bed.'

'It wasn't always in a bed.'

Now her face inched closer to him, her voice dropping to a whisper. 'I don't need to know the details.'

'But I can help you remember.'

Her lips parted. Their faces were so close that he could feel the heat of her breath brushing like the lightest petal against his mouth. And then she closed her eyes tightly, reared away from him and snapped her eyes back open with a glare. 'I don't want to remember, thank you very much.'

He laughed at this blatant lie. The constriction in his trousers burned but he welcomed it. He would bet his favourite house that Orla was suffering the feminine version of his burn. 'Scared you'll remember how good it was?'

'More like I'm afraid to remember how awful it was,' Orla retorted as airily as she could, resisting the urge to cross her legs tightly for fear that he would know *why* she was crossing them.

She'd been about to kiss him. Her mouth had practically salivated in anticipation. The most intimate part of her had throbbed then flooded with a warmth that still tingled acutely.

'The brain is a funny thing, but it does try to protect the body it's encased in,' she added.

Her attempt to stab at the heart of his ego ended in failure. His voice became a sensuous purr that sent fresh tingles careering over her already sensitised skin. 'I can help you remember, *dolcezza*. All you have to do is say the word.'

'And what word would that be? Do I wave my hand in the air, yell out "sex" and you whisk me to bed?' She regretted her flippant remark the moment it left her mouth.

Tonino leaned in even closer, eyes gleaming. 'That sounds good to me. Or you can do what you did on our third night together.'

Orla knew she was taking the bait of the trap he'd laid but was unable to stop herself from whispering, 'What did I do?'

The gleam deepened, the strong nostrils flaring as he stared at her appreciatively and put his mouth to her ear. 'You performed a seductive striptease for me then lay on my bed naked and touched yourself—'

'I did no such thing,' she cut in angrily, rearing away from him. She would *never* do such a thing. Hadn't her grandmother always told her that anything but straight penetrative sex within the confines of marriage was for harlots, the inference being harlots like Orla's mother? For sure, Tonino was the sexiest man she'd ever set eyes on and for sure her body reacted in wanton ways she'd never dreamed of, but to touch herself for his titillation...?

Never.

Please, God, let it not be true.

Now Tonino was the one to rear back. The look he cast her only made her feel more mortified. '*Dio*, you really don't remember, do you?'

The car came to a stop.

Right on cue, Finn woke up.

Cheeks flaming with humiliation, Orla removed Finn from his car seat. She was halfway up the steps of the medical centre for his physiotherapy appointment when she realised she'd failed to put him in his wheelchair and still had him in her arms.

Tonino, Orla decided, was some kind of mind guru. For the third time in two days he'd steamrollered her into doing something she'd thought she would never agree to, in this case, leaving Finn with the duty nurse and letting him take her out to dinner.

He'd had those powers over her from the beginning. When he'd knocked on her hotel door four years ago and asked if he could take her out for coffee the next morning, the automatic refusal that had formed on her tongue had turned into a beaming, 'I would like that.'

She hated that the same excitement thrummed through her veins as it had then. She hated that she'd found herself trying over and over to capture the memories of them making love. And she hated that whenever she caught Tonino's gaze, his knowing glimmer suggested he knew exactly what she was thinking.

She especially hated that she'd spent an age getting ready. This was not a date. This was dinner. A chance for them to talk with privacy about how they were going to manage the future. She'd still spent an inordinate amount of time dithering over what to wear. In the end she'd settled on a pretty long-sleeved rust-coloured blouse and smart, fitted navy trousers, the two items separated by a chunky belt. She'd forgone her usual flat shoes for a pair of black heels. Outfit decided on, she'd then spent an even longer amount of time dithering over how to wear her hair and how much make-up to apply. She'd ended up leaving her hair loose and applying a little eyeliner and mascara, a touch of blusher and a nude lipstick. Dressed up but not overdone. There was no way Tonino could look at her and think she was dressing to attract him.

And yet, the appreciation in his eyes when

she'd greeted him at the front door had almost had her running back up the stairs to change into a nun's habit. Only the fact that she didn't actually possess a nun's habit had stopped her.

'Where are we going?' she asked when she realised they'd left the city and were driving through Ireland's beautiful countryside. That was one thing she missed about her old home in Kerry—the scenery. The home she'd spent her life in had backed onto forest. They had awoken every morning to the sound of birds chirruping. Now she awoke to the sounds of cars hooting impatiently at each other.

'You will see.'

Soon they'd turned up a narrow road lined with woodland. A mile later, the trees thinned and somehow curved into an arch to reveal a sprawling stone structure and immaculately kept sweeping gardens artfully filled with stone and marble benches and ornaments, a vast beautiful pond filled with waterlilies and with a wooden bridge traversing it. Dotted around the main structure were small cottages…

Her heart fluttered with excitement as she asked the question she already knew the answer to. 'Is this Bally House?' The pictures she had seen did not do it justice. It was like driving into a magical fairy tale.

His answering smile was definitely smug. *'Sì.'*

The driver pulled up in the large courtyard. As she climbed out, Orla noticed with a pang the young couple holding hands as they walked slowly over a meandering path, oblivious to anyone but each other under the setting sun.

Her fingers felt as if they'd had magnets inserted into the tips, pulling them towards Tonino's hands. She folded her arms across her chest and rammed her hands between her sides and her arms.

They stepped into a large reception area. Three people working at the desk clocked their entrance and, in unison, straightened. The shortest of them, a middle-aged woman, hurried over to greet them.

'Would you like a drink in the bar or to go straight to your table?' she asked.

'We'll go straight to our table,' Tonino replied. 'Thank you, Lorna.'

He'd been there one night. How could he be on first-name terms with the hotel staff already? Orla wondered in amazement. And, as she followed him over polished-oak flooring through a warren of further reception rooms filled with artful antique furniture and dark leather sofas, she wondered how he knew his way around so well. Did he have an inbuilt satnav?

When they reached the huge dining room, the maître d' greeted Tonino by name and bowed his head respectfully to Orla before leading them to a corner table.

Exposed stone walls, giant fireplaces and thick carpet all drove the feeling of the finest of luxury and yet the restaurant managed to contain the rustic appeal of its setting within it. Each table was set with its own candelabra and she counted six chandeliers hanging from the beamed ceiling.

'Your casement of wine arrived this afternoon,' the maître d' said as he placed leather-bound menus before them. 'Shall I bring you a bottle of it?'

'Yes, and anything Miss O'Reilly wants.'

'Just still water for me, please,' she said.

'Very good.' With another bow, the maître d' turned on his heel and vanished.

Immediately, Orla stopped pretending to read her menu and leaned forward to ask conspiratorially, 'You had your own wine delivered here?'

He looked at her thoughtfully. 'Do you remember that business trip to Tuscany I took four years ago?'

'On my last day in Sicily?' An image flashed in her head of her sitting on the steps of her father's villa. She'd been waiting...

Waiting for what?

Tonino nodded. 'I went to see a run-down monastery ripe for conversion.'

The image disappeared. Orla swallowed moisture into her dry throat. 'Oh?'

'I bought it. I converted it into a hotel and spa and turned the land into a vineyard. Our first wine bottles have just been produced.'

'That's what you've had delivered here?'

'Yes.'

'Wow. I'd heard the management here tried to cater to all their guests' whims but allowing you to have a crate of your own wine...'

'*I'm* the management, Orla.'

Confusion creased her brow.

'I bought Bally House three years ago.' Tonino had no idea why he held his breath after this confession.

A long time passed where all Orla did was stare at him with open-mouthed shock. Then she leaned forward. '*You* own Bally House? But how? Why? When we met you'd never been to Ireland.'

'The way you described your country intrigued me. When Bally House came up for sale, the details were sent to me—I have scouts who look worldwide for investment opportunities—I visited, saw its potential and put an offer in.'

The maître d' returned to the table with the wine bottle in hand. A waiter followed with a bottle of still water.

'Try some of the wine,' Tonino urged. 'Please. I would like to hear your thoughts.'

She pulled a forlorn face. 'Alcohol doesn't agree with me any more.'

'In what way?'

'The first glass of wine I had after the accident went straight to my head. I passed out. I've not dared drink more than a sip of it since.'

'Then try only a sip of this.'

She rolled her slim shoulders then relaxed with a small laugh. 'Okay, but if I don't like it, don't blame me.'

'You will like it.'

The laugh she gave this time was louder and huskier. When he filled a third of the glass with the burgundy liquid, she shook her head and chided, 'Are you trying to get me drunk?'

'It is up to you how much of it you drink.'

Eyes locked on his, she picked the glass up and delicately sniffed the contents. Tonino found himself holding his breath as she put it to her delectable lips and took a sip. Long seconds passed before she swallowed.

'Well?' he asked. Orla was the first person unconnected to his business or the world of wine to try it.

'It's rank.'

'Rank?' The unfamiliar word did not strike him as complimentary.

'Gross. Disgusting. So disgusting that I think I should try a bit more to reinforce just how gross it is.' She put the glass back to her lips.

'You're playing with me,' he accused.

The smile she bestowed him with was the most genuine she'd given him since their eyes had met in the cathedral. It dived straight into his chest and pierced it. She took another small drink, put the glass on the table and tilted her head to say softly, 'It's beautiful.'

'So are you.'

Their eyes held. Something passed between them that sent his pulses soaring.

Only the arrival of the waiter at their table broke it. 'Are you ready to order?'

CHAPTER EIGHT

WHEN ORLA TASTED her starter of cured salmon, crab and smoked roe all wrapped in the most delicate pancake, she thought she'd died and gone to heaven. When she took her first bite of her main course of aged fillet of Irish beef and the shiitake tart accompanying it, she decided that if this was heaven, she wanted to stay. If reaching heaven would allow her to drink Tonino's wine without conking out, then even better. She hadn't been joking when she called it beautiful. It was easily the most delicious wine she'd ever tasted, and she wished with all her heart that she could have more of it.

'Were you not tempted to make the menu more Sicilian?' she asked.

'This hotel could not be more Irish,' he said dryly. 'I don't think a Sicilian theme would work, do you?'

She shrugged. 'I know nothing of hotels and

restaurants. I was just curious. How many hotels do you own?'

'Eighteen. I'm in the process of buying another on the Greek island of Agon. I'm flying there tomorrow to deal with some paperwork.'

'You're leaving tomorrow?' That was *not* disappointment she felt.

'First thing in the morning.' He grinned. 'Are you going to miss me?'

'Like a migraine.'

His laughter filled her ears and sent a warm feeling trickling through her veins. 'I was going to discuss this with you. I will be away for two days. That will give my staff enough time to set up a bedroom for Finn—when I return to Sicily I want Finn to come—'

'That's not possible,' she interrupted. In less than a second, all the warmth in her veins had solidified into ice.

'Why not?' He asked it pleasantly enough, but she detected the underlying warning in his tone.

'It's too soon. He has medication and...'

'There is nothing he has here that he cannot have in Sicily provided we prepare well for it. It will only be for a week.'

'Only a week?' she echoed faintly. Was it her imagination or were the restaurant's stone walls starting to blur and spin? As much as she was enjoying this meal, being apart from Finn for an evening felt as if she'd had a limb removed. How was she supposed to cope for a whole week without him?

'*Sì*. I can clear my schedule for a week so Finn and I can get to know each other but then my schedule is packed with appointments that cannot be rearranged,' he continued as if she hadn't spoken. 'The weekend after that my parents are hosting a party for all the family to meet my sister's new baby—'

'Giulia had another baby?' Orla interrupted again, startled, remembering that four years ago Tonino had been excited for the forthcoming birth of Giulia's first child.

'She had a baby girl last week.'

'You never said.'

He shrugged. 'We have had other things to talk about, *dolcezza*.'

'I know, but a new baby is something to celebrate.' Orla had nearly hit the roof in excitement when Aislin told her she was pregnant.

'And it will be. The party is a good opportunity to introduce Finn to everyone. There will be lots of small children for him to play with including my other nieces and nephews.'

'How many do you have now?' she asked faintly. He'd spun her on the dance floor to face his family while he rebuked her for keeping Finn from them, but that had been the only time since their lives had collided back together that he'd mentioned them.

'Five in total.'

Feeling another headache starting to form, Orla rubbed her temples. 'I don't know if the nurses will be able to travel at such short notice.'

'There are private nurses in Sicily. It will be easy to arrange. Which brings me to my next point—the funding of Finn's medical care.'

'Dante pays for anything not covered by our healthcare system.'

'I thought as much.' His eyes narrowed. 'How did you fund it before you found him?'

'We didn't. It's what made us seek Dante out in the first place.' She took a deep breath and tried to get the panic under control. How could she let Tonino take Finn to Sicily? It was too soon. She wasn't ready to let him go. 'When his father—my father—died, Aislin and I were skint. The insurance company was fighting over any pay-out from the accident. Aislin convinced me I was entitled to some of my father's estate. Neither of us knew he'd gambled most of his wealth away. Once Dante learned about me and Finn he became our knight in shining armour. Before he stepped in, Aislin and I were basically on our own.'

Thinking about the large number of Irish guests at Aislin and Dante's wedding, Tonino found this hard to believe. 'What about the rest of your family?'

'Spectacularly useless.' She rolled her eyes and shook her head but there was no malice in the gestures. 'Most of them live miles away and have their own worries.' To his surprise, she reached for her wine glass and drank a tiny bit more before inhaling deeply and seeming to brace herself. 'Tonino. Please. I'm not trying to be awkward but it's too soon for you to be taking Finn to Sicily.'

'I would say it's too late. I have been incredibly patient, *dolcezza*...'

She snorted inelegantly.

'But Finn has been deprived of half his heritage. It is time for him to learn the Valente half of himself.'

She dropped her stare. When she looked back at him he couldn't tell if it was anguish or anger that was the most prevalent emotion in her eyes. 'Is that what this evening is all about?' she accused. 'A nice meal together to lull me into a false sense of security before you snatch my son from me?'

'You need to get some perspective,' he said coolly.

'Perspective?' She clutched at her hair and looked as if she was preparing to shout at him. Thankfully the waiter arrived at their table to clear their plates away, giving her a few moments to calm herself.

'Tonino, please, just listen to me,' she beseeched. 'Tonight is the first time in two years that I've left Finn for longer than half an hour. I've spent the evening stopping myself from phoning home to check on him every five minutes. I know I must sound selfish, but I can't...' To his shock, tears filled her eyes. She closed them and took another long breath. 'I don't know how I'll cope without him for a whole week. And then to do it all again a week later?'

Cope without him?

Suddenly everything became clear.

Leaning forward, Tonino stared at her until her damp eyes met his. 'Orla, I never said I would take him to Sicily without you.'

Confusion creased her brow. 'Didn't you? But you only spoke about Finn and getting to know him and introducing him to your family and the party and everything.'

He muttered a curse under his breath. 'I want all these things but I cannot believe you would think me cruel enough to take him without you. He hardly knows me. It would terrify him.' And, he could see, destroy Orla. 'You seem to have a habit of assuming the worst about me.'

'I'm sorry...in fairness, you did threaten a

custody battle,' she reminded him. 'It's not an easy thing to forget.'

He drummed his fingers against his wine glass. 'I accept that, but those threats were made in anger and I've assured you since that I don't want to put Finn through that. Stop thinking the worst and accept that, where our son is concerned, you and I are of the same mind—we only want what's best for him.'

She slumped in her chair and pressed her palm to her forehead. 'I can be such an eejit.'

'*Sì,*' he agreed.

A smile unexpectedly formed on his lips as he recalled the first time he'd heard that particular Irish insult from her. They'd been driving in his car—well, not *his* car but one of the staff cars he'd bought for his hotel staff to do their errands in—with the roof down when he'd made a comment about something, he didn't remember what. He did, however, remember Orla lightly punching him on his biceps and calling him an eejit.

That had been one hell of a good day. The sun had blazed as hot as their passion and through it all had been the knowledge that this sweet, funny, beautiful woman had wanted him only for himself. She had wanted Tonino the man, not Tonino Valente the billionaire hotelier. She hadn't wanted to be in his bed to join the Valente dynasty, she hadn't been playing the role of a chess piece taking a strategic move with the ultimate hope of becoming his queen.

She'd just wanted him.

The memories filled him with a warmth that had him reaching out to cover her hand. 'You and Finn come as a package. I accept that. Now you need to accept that I'm part of that package too and that means telling Dante his money isn't needed any more. I'll be paying for everything now.' Before she could protest, he added, 'I'm Finn's father. You two are my responsibility.'

She tugged her hand from his and wrapped her fingers around her glass of water. 'If you want to pay for Finn's care then I won't argue, but I'm not your responsibility.'

'You're the mother of my child.'

'Exactly. I'm not *your* child. I'm an adult. Dante gave me my share of what was left of our father's estate and got his lawyers to make the insurance company pay out. I have money of my own right now.'

'How much?'

'Enough to keep me going for a few years.'

'Marry me and you need never worry about money again.'

She gave a splutter that could have been laughter or exasperation. 'How many times are we going to have this conversation before you get it in your thick head that I'm not going to marry you?'

'My mother assured me throughout my childhood that it's a woman's prerogative to change her mind. I have every intention of changing yours.'

'Good luck with that. I'm a stubborn mule.'

'And I've never been able to resist a challenge.' He poured himself some more wine and contemplated her lazily. Now that he'd put her mind at ease about her travelling to Sicily with Finn, she'd visibly relaxed.

She had the peaceful air about her that he remembered from before and for a moment he could almost imagine they were the same two people they'd been then.

But of course they weren't. He wasn't the same man. And she wasn't the same woman. Her memory was mostly repaired and she looked the same as she'd done four years ago but her movements had lost much of their old grace. She tired easily. Even the way she ate, holding her knife and fork so tightly, cutting her food with such concentration…

'You were six months pregnant when the accident happened?' he asked carefully.

She nodded. A sad smile curved her cheeks. 'Finn was born by emergency Caesarean. He spent eight weeks in Intensive Care. They didn't think he was going to make it.' A spark flashed in her eyes. 'But our son's a fighter. He proved them all wrong.'

Feeling his stomach clench then churn, he took a moment to ask, 'And you? Was there a danger you wouldn't have made it?'

She hesitated before giving the tiniest of nods. 'I was in a coma for three weeks and then under sedation for another month. But I'm fine now,' she hastened to add. 'And things are massively better with Finn too. We know what we're dealing with and I always think that's half the battle.'

'Who looked after him while you were in hospital? Aislin?' She'd already said Aislin had been the one to register Finn's birth.

She gave another nod. 'She quit her degree—quit her life—to look after us both. When I finally came home, she taught me how to care for him. Finn is my miracle. Aislin is my angel.'

She'd already described Dante as her knight in shining armour. So what did that make Tonino?

He thought it better not to ask.

'Where was your mother in all this?'

An emotion he couldn't determine flittered over her face. 'I haven't seen my mother in seven years. As far as I know she's in San Francisco.'

'She wasn't there for you?'

She picked up her wine glass and stared at the burgundy liquid. 'I don't think she's ever been there for me. Aislin and I spent more time with our grandparents next door than we ever did with her. Two weeks after Aislin finished high school our mother scarpered to Asia and never came back.'

Even the edge to her voice, never mind her words, struck Tonino like a blow. It was a tone he'd never heard before and he peered closely at her. 'Never?'

The misery he witnessed on her face struck him like a second blow.

She swallowed before answering. 'Put it this way, she's never met Finn.'

A grandmother who'd never met her only grandchild? Surely not? 'What about when you were in the coma and he was in Intensive Care?'

'She texted Aislin for updates.'

That struck him even harder than Orla's other revelations.

He imagined her hooked to machines, locked in her own head, unable to communicate, unable to respond to anything and his heart swelled so greatly it became an effort to breathe. To think her own mother had abandoned her to that fate without one single visit defied all humanity.

Little wonder Orla struggled to trust and open up to people. Of the two people whose job had been to love her and raise her, one had rejected her in the womb, the other doing the bare essentials until she could leave for good.

His throat moved before he asked hoarsely, 'How did the accident happen?'

'I don't remember.' She shook her head as if clearing her ears. 'That period is still a blur. I don't even remember where I was going. I know it must have been somewhere important because there was a bad storm and I'm not comfortable driving in bad weather. I know I had a collision with a Transit van but I don't remember anything of the accident itself.' Suddenly she grinned. It made her whole face light up. 'Probably just as well. I'm terrible around blood.'

He returned the grin, glad of the lightening of mood.

But he couldn't escape the feeling in his guts that there was more to Orla's injuries than she was sharing with him.

As they left the cosy warmth of the Bally House Hotel restaurant, the breezy chill in the air outside came as something of a shock, especially as Orla had neglected to bring a jacket with her. She looked up at the sky and was disappointed to find all the stars hidden under thick cloud. Summer was practically over, she thought wistfully.

Yawning as the long day finally caught up

with her, she rubbed her arms for warmth. Eagle-eyed Tonino noticed and removed his charcoal suit jacket and placed it on her shoulders.

'You don't have to do that,' she protested.

'I'm not cold,' he answered smugly.

And now, neither was she. Tonino's jacket was so big and contained so much warmth that it enveloped her body like a giant hug.

Its warmth came from his body heat.

The driver noticed their approach and opened the back door for her.

She climbed inside and was about to reluctantly give Tonino his jacket back when he slid in beside her.

'You don't need to escort me back,' she chided, smothering another yawn.

'I want to see you home safely.'

The driver pulled away.

'Don't be silly.' She smothered yet another yawn. She was utterly exhausted and yet…

Alone with Tonino in the confines of the back seat of his car, the partition between them and the driver raised…

Suddenly she was aware of the beats of her heart and the thickening of her blood.

Suddenly she was aware of Tonino's cologne dancing through her airwaves. The urge to rub her cheek into his jacket still draped over her shoulders became almost irresistible.

And suddenly she was aware of his thigh pressed against hers.

She should move away from him. Edge herself to the door. Create a distance.

She knew what she *should* do. Her body had other thoughts and was refusing to take orders from her brain. She cleared her throat. 'You've only got to come all the way back and it's not like you'll see Finn—he'll be asleep.' The car's interior darkened as they drove through the thick woodland. 'You should get some sleep too before all that travelling you've got to do...'

His hand closed over hers, stifling her words. It felt very different from the way he'd covered her hand in the restaurant. That had been for reassurance during what had proved to be a difficult yet ultimately necessary conversation. Since then, they'd spoken only of light, forgettable things and yet, instinctively, she knew she would remember every word exchanged.

If only she could remember those last missing pieces. What had happened with her father was becoming clearer. She'd waited on his doorstep for his housekeeper to find him. She didn't need the actual memory to know the housekeeper had returned with the message that he didn't want to see her. Orla knew it in her heart.

The memory she most wanted back was the accident. Where had she been going? She'd been two hours from home on the main road to Dublin…

Her desperate thoughts, barriers to help her pretend that the electricity bouncing over skin wasn't really happening, dissolved. The weight and warmth of Tonino's skin against hers made coherent thought impossible.

'I would sleep much better if I was in your bed,' he murmured.

A loose breath escaped her throat, barely audible above the humming in her ears.

She should move her hand from his and move her body away too. Instead she found her fingers lacing through his. When his thigh pressed tighter against hers and his shoulder leaned against hers, she smothered a gasp at the throb that pulsed through her abdomen and sent an ache rippling through the rest of her.

She didn't dare utter another word. She didn't dare look at him.

There was an excitement in her belly that was both new and yet familiar. She didn't remember the feelings but knew, in the same instinctive way she'd known she was pregnant and that Finn's father was Sicilian before the memories came back, that she'd felt them before.

His fingers squeezed then unlaced from hers to rest lightly on her thigh. The heat from his touch fizzed right into her veins.

Her fingers spread themselves over *his* thigh before her brain could compute what they were doing.

Slowly, slowly, his fingers crept upwards, gently caressing until they reached the apex of her thighs. She squeezed reflexively and gasped when his thumb brushed over the material covering her femininity.

She found herself helpless to stop her fingers slowly dragging themselves up the muscular thighs, closer and closer to...

Orla swallowed hard when the tip of her finger brushed something solid.

Dimly she was aware that Tonino's breaths had become heavy. In the echoes of her mind she heard her own breaths too, ragged bursts as erratic as her heartbeats.

She pressed her pelvis against his hand.

He shifted so his chest pressed against her breast. His mouth pressed against the top of her head. Hot breaths permeated through her skin, darts of need careering through her veins and down to her liquid core.

Feeling drugged, she turned her face up to his. The heat swirling in his dark hooded eyes only heightened the sensations that had taken control of her body. The whispers of his breaths danced over her lips.

He covered her hand and gently slid it to cover

the bulge between his legs. A thrill so powerful shot through her that her breath hitched, and it took a moment for her to register his hand no longer covered hers but had moved to her shoulder. Slowly it brushed down, over her breasts and stomach to the part of her body now aching with torment.

And then the warmth against her lips changed. It solidified, flesh forming from the air…

Tonino's mouth was grazing against hers…

This time she could not hold back the gasp that flew from her throat. The firm pressure of Tonino's lips against hers muffled the sound but did nothing to muffle the shaking of her right knee.

When his mouth moved she found her own mouth moving in time. She found her chest straining to him…*all* the cells in her body were straining to him. She barely noticed he'd undone the button of her trousers until he slipped his hand into the loosened space and burrowed into her knickers. Her gasp was muffled again by the delicious pressure of his mouth. Her mouth flooding with moisture, Orla cupped his cheek and tried to hold on to herself but it was a battle she'd lost before she'd started. A thick finger slid over her swollen nub, making her gasp again and turning her breaths into shallow pants that echoed around her. Wantonly, she pressed against the finger, heightening the sensation, and moaned into his mouth.

Her fingers moved from his cheek to cradle his head and she closed her eyes, letting her body and Tonino's clever manipulations guide her responses.

Clinging tightly to him, their breaths merged together, she bucked against him with increasing urgency until the pleasure consumed her in its entirety and she was whimpering against him, her face burrowed in his neck, sensation that felt as if it had been dipped in nectar flooding her throbbing pelvis.

She had no idea how long it took for reality to snake its way into her delirious consciousness.

She opened her eyes.

That was Tonino's neck her face was pressed against.

That was Tonino's strong arm holding her so tightly and protectively against him.

That was his heartbeat thudding through his chest and reverberating in her ear.

That was his hand…

That was *her* hand…

Suddenly awash with mortification, Orla snatched her hand away from his crotch and yanked his hand away from hers and turned from him to fasten and straighten her clothes.

Tonino didn't make a sound or a movement

until, moments later, the car came to a stop and he shifted beside her.

She swallowed and kept her gaze fixed forward, afraid to look at him.

How could she ever look at him again?

'We have arrived, *dolcezza*,' he said huskily. His breath danced against her cheek. She closed her eyes.

A finger touched her chin.

Her heart jumped.

The air around her shifted again. Tonino had moved even closer.

There was not an inch of her skin that didn't reawaken. Anticipation bubbled but still she kept her eyes closed.

The finger on her chin skimmed lightly over her cheek, reaching her ear. A hand plunged into her hair. Fresh tingles capered joyously on her sensitised skin.

'Are you going to invite me in?' he whispered into her ear.

'What?' Dazed, she opened her eyes, her stare immediately captured in the swirling depths of Tonino's hungry gaze.

He captured her chin again and kissed her. Kissed her properly. Kissed her so hard and so thoroughly that the heat rebuilding deep inside her liquefied her bones as it bubbled to the surface.

The hand in her hair drifted down her back. 'Invite me in,' he whispered against her lips before crushing her mouth again. His hand reached her bottom and squeezed then ran over her thigh, squeezing and massaging, his mouth devouring her, sensation running amok through her.

It would be so easy to invite him into her home and lead him up to her room rather than Finn's...

And just like that, sanity reared its gloriously ugly head.

Fixing their son's image in her head and focusing only on that, she placed her hands on his chest and pushed him off. 'No.'

He sat back, breathing heavily. 'No, what?'

'No, I am not going to invite you in.' Heart hammering furiously, she groped for the door handle but found herself all fingers and thumbs.

A large, warm, hard body lightly covered hers. 'Let me,' he murmured. And then he opened the door.

Before she could escape, he palmed her cheek and brushed his lips against hers one last time. 'I will see you in a few days,' he murmured.

'Grand,' she answered in what she intended to be a tart fashion, but which came out all breathless.

She felt breathless. Tonino was the only man she had ever desired and it made her want to weep that the old feelings were still there inside her but impossible to fulfil.

Eyes glittering, he brought her hand to his mouth and grazed a kiss against her knuckles. 'I will count the hours.'

CHAPTER NINE

ORLA LOOKED OUT of the car window, eyes straining for the first view of Tonino's home.

Finn was beside himself with excitement. If her little trouper could have packed his own case, he would have done it within seconds of her telling him about their trip. Finn hadn't immediately embraced Tonino as he'd done with Dante and she wondered if it was because Finn detected the threat Tonino posed to their family life. Whatever the reason behind it—and she wouldn't ask unless it became a problem, as she didn't want to feed ideas to him that might not already be there—she was glad he was excited to be back in Sicily and excited to be seeing his father.

There was no point denying the butterflies rampaging in her belly were testament to her own excitement. The leaping of her heart at every alert from her phone these past three days was testament too. The few times the alerts had come from Tonino…quite frankly she was surprised to find her heart still secure behind her ribs.

Hearing his voice down the line had had the effect of turning the thousands of miles between them into nothing. The deep tones would dive through her ears and heat her veins, sensitising her skin as acutely as if she were in the back of his car with him again, a recent memory that had had her clutching her cheeks in mortification so many times these past three days it was a wonder she hadn't worn her cheekbones down.

This was how it had been for her four years ago, Orla turning into a walking tinderbox of feverish heat and heightened emotions. Her emotions were far more yo-yo-like than they had been then. Nothing could come of these feelings. She wanted to trust him but how could she after all the lies? And even if she found a way to trusting him, Tonino didn't want *her*. He wanted their son. He might still desire her, but one look at her naked body would extinguish it. If she could hardly bring herself to look at her own reflection how could she expect him to react to it with anything but horror?

The winding, narrow road that they'd been driving on for the past five minutes, through fields of crops ready to be harvested, peaked. In the distance rose a salmon-coloured stone chateau.

Orla cleared her throat and pointed. 'Look, Finn. That's your daddy's house.' She could not say where this certainty came from, but she would bet her own house that it belonged to Tonino.

Finn strained against the restraints of his car seat, trying to get a decent view.

The closer they got, the more the chateau—at least, that was what she called it in her head—emerged, but it wasn't until they drove through a high stone arch into an enormous courtyard that she fully appreciated its vast magnificence. The chateau surrounded the courtyard, which could double as a car park if the need arose, in a square. In the centre of the courtyard stood a fountain with a trio of cherubs in it, the water squirting from a certain part of the cherubs' anatomy that had Finn squealing with laughter when he spotted it.

Baskets of flowers hung on the chateau's walls, random palm trees adding additional colour, and Tonino...

Orla blinked and looked again.

Her heart soared and caught in her throat.

Tonino had emerged from nowhere, as if he'd slithered out of the chateau's walls or, as was more likely, become flesh from a marble statue, Adonis brought to life. Unlike the marble statue of the naughty cherubs, Tonino was dressed, insofar as a pair of black shorts and a lazy grin could be considered as dressed.

The driver opened the door and, as Orla carried Finn out, Tonino walked over to them. The late afternoon sun beamed down and cast his bare chest in a hazy glow.

She remembered pressing her lips to that chest and inhaling the musky scent of his skin. She remembered rubbing her cheeks against the thick hair spread across it and marvelling at the contrasts between them, his masculinity and her femininity, as different as night from day yet the two of them coming together...

Their coming together was still a blank.

His dreamy chocolate eyes caught hers. His lazy grin widened before he planted a kiss right on her lips. Immediately her senses were assailed with the scents of salt, muskiness and the faint remnants of Tonino's cologne. The stubble of his unshaved face rubbed against her cheek and when he broke the kiss as abruptly as he'd formed it, she had to stop her fingers from pressing against her tender, stubble-assaulted skin. She had to stop herself from swaying into him and pulling him back for another.

Before she had the chance to compose a greeting that didn't make her sound like a brain-dead eejit, Tonino had lifted Finn from her arms.

'How was the journey?' He rubbed his nose

against Finn's in an affectionate gesture that sent her heart soaring all over again.

Only the good Lord knew how she untied her tongue to answer. 'Fine.'

He looked back at her and shifted Finn on his hip. 'My apologies for not sending my plane to you.'

She forced her vocal cords to cooperate. 'I cannot believe you're apologising for making us travel first class.'

'It is an inconvenience for you.'

The serious way in which he declared this made her snort with laughter. 'Seriously? First class an inconvenience? And you say *I* need to get some perspective?'

For a long moment Tonino stared at her, enjoying the way the sunlight bounced on her thick dark hair and injected it with strands of gold and red. 'You look beautiful.'

As beautiful and as fresh as any flower his gardener coaxed into bloom on his estate.

Tonino had arrived back in Sicily a few hours earlier than expected. He would have flown to Ireland to collect them, but they'd already left for the airport. Finding himself pacing the chateau's corridors and getting in the way of his live-in staff, he'd gone for a swim but quickly found himself bored so had resorted to playing tennis with his ball-launcher machine as an opponent. That had used up much of his latent energy but not all of it, not with the promise of Orla and his son arriving at any moment feeding him energy as quickly as he wore it out.

Gazing at her now, he felt as if he'd done no exercise at all. His veins still thrummed. His skin and loins still buzzed with anticipation.

The memory of what had taken place in the back of his car had shadowed his every waking moment since.

The three days away from Orla had passed slowly. A snail could have passed the time more quickly.

It had been the same when she'd disappeared four years ago. Life had suddenly gone from passing at breakneck speed to a crawl.

This time, he was certain the slowing of time had been because he'd been parted from his son. Already his feelings for Finn ran deep. They were feelings he'd never had before, different from any other emotion. Far different from the feelings he had for Finn's mother. There was a purity to his feelings for Finn, a semi-conscious knowledge that for this child he would be prepared to kill to keep him safe. He would never allow his son to feel that the family name and Tonino's pride meant more than Finn's happiness. He would support his son and love him unconditionally.

His feelings for Orla were far more complicated. He hated her for keeping him in the dark about the pregnancy but relished being in her company. He wanted to punish her for her lies. He wanted to worship the body that had created something so special for them. He desired her. He fantasised about her. Orla being back in his life had set off a charge in his veins that time had dulled. He'd forgotten it could be so strong. She was the only woman the charge had scorched him for.

Dio, he longed to throw her on his bed, rip her clothes off and plunder that beautiful body. He longed to hear the soft moans that had once fallen from her lips. He longed to hear her pleas for more.

But this Orla was not the Orla of four years ago. That Orla had been impulsive. She had thrown caution to the wind and embraced the desire that had caught them both in its snare. For a short shameless passage of time she had sunk into the desire still binding them so tightly together. The way she had come undone for him had blown his mind. Orla had always blown his mind.

Four years ago they had been dynamite together and that explosive chemistry still bubbled strongly. If desire alone could bind Orla to him he'd have already won. But this Orla was a mother. Motherhood had made her cautious. She thought with her brain rather than be led by her desires. To get what he wanted, namely Finn permanently in his life, he needed to seduce her brain. He needed to make her feel that his home could be *their* home. Because to achieve what he wanted he needed to bring Orla into his life permanently too.

The next morning, Orla closed Finn's bedroom door carefully and put her finger to her lips to remind her son to be quiet.

She needn't have bothered with silence. No sooner had she taken her first step than Tonino's bedroom door opened.

She could scream. Yet again he'd caught her at the crack of dawn looking as though she'd been dragged through a gooseberry bush backwards.

He caught the look on her face and grinned. 'How many times do I have to tell you that I'm an early riser before you believe me?'

'No one gets up this early voluntarily, not unless they're a three-year-old child.'

'Why doesn't the nurse get up with him?' he asked when they reached the kitchen, a space that was double the size of the ground floor of her old house. The scent of fresh coffee filled the room. So tantalising was it that Orla suddenly found herself craving a coffee for the first time in years.

'It's not her job.' Tonino had been as good as his word at employing wraparound care for Finn here in Sicily. The nurses he'd employed worked shifts and were unobtrusive, present if needed but fading into the background when not required. They also spoke excellent English and had cared for children with cerebral palsy before.

'Her job is whatever you require it to be.' He opened a cupboard door. 'It's in the contract.'

'Sure, but getting up and feeding my child is my job. Caring for my child is my job.' And a job it had taken eighteen months of blood, sweat and tears to achieve.

He shut the cupboard he'd been looking through and opened the next one. 'When was the last time you slept later than six a.m.?'

Her last night in the rehabilitation centre. 'Years ago... What are you looking for?'

'Finn's cereal. I instructed my housekeeper to buy some for him.'

'Where do you usually keep cereal?'

'I have no idea.'

'But it's your kitchen.'

'It's my chef's kitchen,' he corrected. 'I never cook, but I'm not a breakfast eater so she doesn't

usually start until ten. I'll get her to start earlier while—'

'Don't you dare. There's no need for the entire
household to be up early just because of Finn.'

'What if you want food too?'

'I rarely eat more than a slice of toast in the
morning. I hardly need a cordon bleu chef to butter it for me.' A thought occurred to her. 'If the
chef hasn't started yet, who made the coffee?'

'It's on a timer. If you hunt for cups you'll find
them somewhere. I have mine black.' Tonino
grinned, then made a noise that sounded like
the Sicilian equivalent of *aha!* and pulled the
box of cereal out of the cupboard.

A warm sensation flooded Orla's chest and
belly when Tonino, after rooting through a
dozen other cupboards, pulled out a plastic
bowl with dinosaurs on it. Her heart bloomed
when he opened a drawer and removed a plastic spoon, also with dinosaurs on. He filled the
bowl, added the milk and joined them at the
table, where Orla had put Finn in the brand-new
high chair Tonino had bought him and laid their
cups of coffee down.

A strange contentment settled in her as she
sat back and sipped the delicious coffee. Despite
the palatial proportions of the chateau and its
kitchen, there was something heartwarming to

witness the uber-masculine Tonino feed cereal on a dinosaur spoon into a three-year-old's mouth.

'Seeing as you are averse to nurses caring for our son in anything but a medical capacity, do you not think it makes sense for me to take on the early morning parental role while you are here?' he asked, catching her eye briefly. He adopted a cajoling tone. 'Think of those extra hours in bed.'

'I'll think about it,' she muttered, knowing full well there was nothing to think about but also knowing Tonino would never understand her feelings on the subject. He'd been deprived of their son for the first three years of Finn's life but he hadn't known about it because he hadn't known of Finn's existence. He hadn't *missed* Finn because how could you miss something you'd never had? Orla had spent eighteen months fighting her own body just to be well enough to hold her child, missing him with every breath she took. Finn had been the focus she'd needed to get through those dark, terrifying days and even darker nights. Getting up early to feed Finn his breakfast was a privilege that she would never take for granted but she couldn't share this with Tonino.

How could she trust that he wouldn't use her injuries against her in a custody battle?

She wanted to trust him but until she could, she would try to keep the extent of her injuries from him.

The early morning turned into a sunny day lazily spent exploring the grounds of Tonino's magnificent estate. After lunch on the terrace, Orla sat on a sunlounger by the huge swimming pool, shades on, a sheer navy kaftan covering her body and the swimsuit she would never get wet, and watched her son squeal with delight to be dipped into the fresh water by his father.

The joy on Tonino's face sliced through her too, just as acutely.

She'd been so certain that not telling him until after the birth was right. She remembered taking the pregnancy test and minutes later searching his name online to discover his engagement to Sophia was over, her heart thumping. She'd been thankful that she wouldn't have to break the Sicilian woman's heart a second time but this confirmation of Tonino's sudden 'availability' had not made Orla feel any better about her predicament. If anything it had made her feel worse. With no fiancée at his side, there would be nothing to hold him off launching a custody battle. Orla's father had wanted nothing to do with her but Tonino was not her father. Tonino wanted children. Lots of them.

He had the wealth and connections to get custody of the tiny life in her belly. She'd made the conscious decision to wait until after the birth before telling him. That would allow her a relatively stress-free pregnancy and allow her to register her child as an Irish citizen and to put whatever protection in place she could to stop him using his connections against her. She remembered being terrified. In her mind she'd painted Tonino as a monster. She'd painted him as a cheat, a liar and an all-powerful deity with the ability to snap his fingers and snatch her baby from her.

She'd forgotten that he was a flesh and blood man. She'd forgotten that their time together had been wonderful because *he'd* been wonderful... No, she hadn't forgotten. She'd just convinced herself it had all been an act while he'd had his fun with her.

Guilt that Finn and Tonino never had the chance to be father and son from birth gnawed at her. She remembered carrying the guilt in her...

A new memory flashed in her mind and sent her heart racing anew, of searching Tonino's name online and finding a picture of him and a new woman. She'd effectively cyber-stalked him, she suddenly remembered. She'd searched his name most days.

She remembered Finn reacting to her reaction

to Tonino and the new woman by giving a huge kick. She must have seen that picture shortly before the accident because Finn had only really started kicking her belly with gusto a few weeks before it.

Orla thought hard, trying to remember who the new woman had been, but the memory refused to form. It would come in its own time. The memories refused to be forced, especially the significant ones.

Orla thought again about that woman later that evening while soaking in the bath. Tonino had announced that he was taking her out for dinner, leaving the duty nurse in charge of Finn. He'd refused to listen to a word of argument against it.

They'd dined on his rooftop veranda the night before, a relaxed meal under a starry sky with the waves of the Tyrrhenian Sea a distant roar.

But the relaxed vibe had been a lie. Orla had spent the evening with a kaleidoscope of large-winged butterflies dancing a storm in her belly. Every time their eyes had met she'd been certain he'd been remembering what had happened in the back of his car. She'd been on tenterhooks for him to allude to it or make a move on her, but when she'd announced at ten p.m. that she was tired and going to bed, he'd inclined his head, raised his glass and wished her a good night.

She'd walked away feeling the burn of his stare scorching her, then crawled into bed unsure whether she was relieved or frustrated.

She should not feel so damned excited at the thought of being alone with him. The dancing butterflies in her belly and the buzz of anticipation bouncing over her skin were traps.

She must remember that Tonino had an ulterior motive in taking her out for dinner just as he had an ulterior motive with everything he did. That ulterior motive was Finn. The incredible effort Tonino was making for her to feel at home and at ease, the beautiful bedroom he'd appointed for her with the triple-aspect windows and private bathroom Cleopatra would consider die-worthy, the walk-in wardrobe filled with brand-new clothing specially selected by a personal shopper under Tonino's instructions especially for her...

She must not let her head be swayed by it all because she knew exactly what he was doing it for—he was making her see how great it would be to marry him. He was making her see all the things he could give her and all the perks she would receive by being his wife. He thought those things would impress her and turn her head. He didn't know her head didn't need turning. It had been turned four years ago and she'd never got over it.

Ultimately, it was Finn he wanted, not Orla. He was just using her as a means to have his son in his life permanently. She couldn't blame him for it.

By the time she'd dressed in a scoop-neck silver dress that fell to her knees and had the requisite long sleeves, and a pair of black glittery heels, she stared at her reflection. She stared at the mirror for so long she half expected a voice to emerge from it.

What would the voice say? Would it laugh at her and say that it didn't matter how she looked with clothes on because any sexual interest Tonino had for her would be extinguished like a candle if he saw her naked?

A part of her thought she should go knocking on his door, whip her dress up to expose the scars and brazenly say, 'There you go. Still fancy me, do you?'

If she couldn't bear to look at her scars herself, how could she ever trust Tonino enough to see them and not use them as a weapon against her?

CHAPTER TEN

THE NIGHT THAT unfolded was one of the best of Orla's life. Tonino drove them in a tiny vintage car that must have been older than the pair of them combined to Palermo, where they dined in the tiniest restaurant she had ever set foot in, which held the grand total of eight tables. Despite its diminutive proportions, the restaurant had a zest to it that could have lifted the lowest of spirits. Loud but not overbearing music pulsed from walls adorned with clever and funny artwork. The food...

'It's just as well I'm not a fussy eater,' she confided when the music dipped low enough for Tonino to hear. The restaurant did not provide a menu. It served three courses of whatever the chef had dreamt up that day, take it or leave it. Having eaten her first course, the most divinely cooked octopus served on a pea and mint broth, with the largest langoustine she'd ever seen accompanying it, she was firmly in the 'take it' camp.

'That's why I brought you here.' He grinned, making her already noodly bones soften even more. Under the subtle lighting, his handsome features had become more defined. With his magnificent body snug in black chinos and a charcoal shirt open at the neck, it was all she could do not to salivate. The man was a walking stick of testosterone.

Tonino was glad he'd followed his instincts and brought Orla here rather than one of Palermo's classier restaurants. This place was one of Sicily's hidden gems, a restaurant that operated on a word-of-mouth basis. If the owner didn't want you there, reserving a table was impossible. If the owner liked you, reserving a table with only hours' notice was easy.

He'd guessed Orla would prefer the informality here but also relish the opportunity to dress up. Four years ago, when she'd been short of money, she'd made an effort with her appearance. Orla was a woman with an eye for fashion, her clothes back then cheap but stylish. She still had that eye but the quality had markedly increased to reflect her increased bank balance.

Time, he was learning, had changed Orla, yet dig beneath the surface and the fundamental essence of who she was remained the same.

Life had dealt her the severest of blows and she was still picking the pieces of it up. He needed to make her see that, together, the pieces could be mended far more effectively than if she remained alone. He needed to make himself indispensable to her and Finn.

While they ate their second course of spaghetti and clams, the music being piped through the restaurant was turned off and a violin quartet appeared. Instead of playing the classical music all the diners anticipated, they tapped their feet and drove straight into a rock classic.

Orla clapped her hands and grinned widely, clearly loving the twist.

'You like?' he murmured, thinking for the hundredth time that evening how beautiful she looked.

She nodded enthusiastically. 'Very much.'

Picking up her fork, she twirled some spaghetti around it and popped it in her mouth, all the while her shoulders danced along to the rock beats.

Tonino found his attention caught with Orla rather than the entertainment. She held his attention like no one else. She always had.

She began nodding her head in time to the music along with her shoulders and absently tucked a lock of her dark hair behind a dainty ear.

He inhaled deeply then exhaled slowly.

He remembered her performing similar moves four years ago at a beachside reggae bar he'd taken her to one evening when he'd decided they needed a short break from his bedroom for food. As his cooking skills consisted entirely of opening packets, and as he hadn't at that point been ready to confess his true identity and so couldn't order a member of his household staff over to his apartment to whip up a four-course meal for them, he'd taken her out, intending to find a semi-decent restaurant. The music pumping from the reggae bar had made Orla's beautiful face widen into a beam and they'd ended up there, sitting at a wooden table on the beach, a blanket covering their laps against the sea breeze, drinking mojitos and sharing a large basket of chips.

It was a memory that had stayed with him. When he thought of the dates he'd been on in his life, that had been by far the best. The simplicity of the setting mixed with the growing realisation that Orla's feelings for him were entirely for *him*...

He wouldn't rewrite history by denying that he'd been a player until his engagement to Sophia. Women had flocked to him and he'd welcomed their attentions while not being under the least illusion that their interest wasn't in part to do with his wealth. If he'd come from a poor family, many of them—Sophia included—would not have looked twice at him.

Orla had huddled under that blanket sharing chips with him, oblivious that he was worth more than a small nation.

If he could turn back time and re-enact history, he would return to that night and tell her the truth of who he was. His mistake had been to not trust her with the truth. He'd been afraid the truth would change how she was with him.

He should have realised that night that his wealth would mean little to her. For Orla, money was a means to an end. Her brother's wealth had been welcome only for what it could do to improve Finn's life. Orla didn't value possessions. She valued family. She valued those she loved.

Driving them back home, Tonino opened a window to get some fresh air into his lungs. He felt lightheaded even though he hadn't touched a drop of alcohol.

Awareness throbbed through him, his mind busy recalling the way she'd wiggled her shoulders to the music; he shot surreptitious glances at her, catching the surreptitious glances she kept shooting back at him... So shot was his concentration that it was a miracle they made it back in one piece.

He brought the car to a stop in the courtyard.

A member of his staff would park it in the underground garage for him.

For a long time they just sat there, the only sound their individual breaths.

He turned to face her at the exact moment she turned to face him. The soft lighting of the courtyard's perimeter cast her in an ethereal shadow that made his lungs tighten along with his loins at the beauty before him.

He reached out to capture a lock of her hair in his fingers.

She stilled, eyes wide on his as if in a trance.

'Have I told you how beautiful you look tonight?' he whispered, releasing the lock of hair to trace his fingers around the rim of her ear.

She shivered at his touch. Her breathing deepened.

Lowering his tone to a purr, he spoke into her hair. 'I have spent the night fantasising about us making love.'

Orla knew Tonino's seductive words and tone were deliberate. His voice had always been an aphrodisiac to her, something he'd taken full advantage of four years ago and which she knew he would not hesitate to use as a weapon again. Her shameful lack of resistance was her own fault.

She tried to breathe, tried to grit her teeth in a form of mental defence, all the while praying, *Please don't touch my body...*

Her aching body begged to differ. Her aching body craved his touch.

When he'd touched her in the back of his car she'd melted into butter.

His finger drifted down her neck to the top of her chest then skimmed lightly, almost nonchalantly, over a breast.

Her insides became liquid and she instinctively pressed the tops of her thighs together, a motion she knew didn't escape his attention. *Nothing* escaped Tonino Valente's attention.

His hot breath whispered through the strands of her hair to burn her scalp. 'We should go in.'

She swallowed and instead of the bright, 'Yes, that's an excellent idea, I'm tired and want to go to bed. Alone. See you in the morning!' she intended, all she managed was something that sounded like, 'Hmm?'

'I said we should go inside…unless you want me to make love to you right here in the car in the middle of the courtyard?'

The liquid inside her heated to unbearable levels. The finger that had skimmed her breast had settled on its underside and was making the lightest circular motions that had her wanting to grab his hand and place it over her breast properly. She wanted to feel his hand there without the barrier of clothes, to feel the heady sensations that had so enraptured her all those years ago.

While her body's responses contradicted everything in her brain, his hand swept over her belly then left her body altogether to unlock her seat belt.

For a moment all she could do was stare into his hooded eyes before the tiniest smile curved on his firm lips and she was suffused in his scent as he leaned over her to open her door.

She got out of the car, her legs like overcooked spaghetti, a different kind of weakness than she usually felt in her limbs. This weakness was nothing to do with her brain. It was all to do with Tonino. Her legs would have felt like spaghetti even without the after-effects of the accident still grabbing at her.

Orla stared up at the black night sky and prayed for the strength to resist this undeniable attraction.

Attraction? If her tongue weren't so tied to the roof of her mouth she would laugh at this pathetic description of the powerful feelings engulfing her.

All the years when she'd tried so hard to remember his name, his face had haunted both her dreams and her waking hours. Her first dream of him after the accident, around the time the doctors had ended her sedation, had been so vivid and real that if she'd been able to get off the bed and walk she would have stalked every inch of the hospital for him.

The accident had wiped his name from her memory bank. It had wiped their time together. It had wiped Sophia's confrontation with her and Orla's discovery of his lies.

The one thing it hadn't wiped, apart from the image of his face, was her feelings for him. But only in her dreams had she dared let those feelings out.

Her heart thumping hard against her ribs, she walked beside him into the chateau and slipped her shoes off. There was not a sound to be heard within the thick stone walls.

Not until they reached the sleeping quarters did she manage to untie her tongue. 'I need to check on Finn.'

She turned the handle of her son's bedroom door and slipped inside. The night light in the corner of the room gave just enough illumination for her to see him sleeping peacefully. The adjoining door to the nurse's room was ajar. Loud snores could be heard from it.

Orla watched her son sleep until the thuds of her heart settled into a gentle rhythm. She crept silently back out, her heart lifting right back to a canter when she found Tonino with his back against the corridor wall, arms loosely crossed over his chest, waiting for her.

Their eyes met. His chest rose.

Her throat caught.

Long, electrified moments passed before Tonino unfolded his arms. Straightening, he took a step towards her.

Her bare feet refused her brain's order to move into the safety of her bedroom, remaining rooted to the terracotta floor.

Two more steps and the distance between them had closed.

A muscular arm hooked around her waist and pulled her flush against him.

She gasped and gazed up at the face that had haunted her dreams for so, so long. Another long, electrified stare passed between them.

She gasped again as she was lifted off her feet, a gasp smothered by the firm, sensuous mouth she had kissed a thousand times in her dreams crushing her lips.

Oh, but this was a kiss that could turn a nun's head, never mind a love-starved Irishwoman whose heart had been given to, then broken by, the only man her body had ever ached for. A thousand brand-new feelings erupted in her and, wrapping her arms around his neck, she returned the kiss with all the passion in her soul, scraping her fingers down his nape as their tongues collided and their mouths moulded into one.

Heat fizzed through her veins as her every atom made a collective sigh that had her tightening her hold on him.

Tonino held her just as tightly. Only when they finally came up for air did he remove an arm from her waist and reach out for the door handle, pushing it open before wrapping the arm back around her.

Orla found herself being half carried into an intensely masculine bedroom. The tips of her toes swished gracefully over thick carpet until she was twisted around and the backs of her legs met resistance in the form of a humongous four-poster bed, which her bottom fell onto.

Immediately he sank down to kneel on the floor before her. Tonino was so tall that with him kneeling and her sitting on the bed, they became the same height.

Large hands cupped her cheeks, dark brown eyes swirling with desire pulsed straight into her. He breathed heavily. *'Amore mio...'* he muttered thickly against her lips, before plundering her mouth anew, his kisses feverish and wet and fierce with intensity.

Another rush of sensory feelings exploded in her. It was as if all her passion for Tonino had been locked away in a box similar to the box that had contained her memories of him, waiting for him to prise the lid open with a kiss like the prince from a fairy tale.

The fever in Tonino's kisses was matched by the fever in her response. She felt drugged. Her aching body craved his touch and craved to touch *him*, to feel the bristles of his chest hair against her cheek. She wanted to rub her nose into it and bite at the brown nipples as she *knew* she'd done before.

Her fingers unbuttoned his shirt so expertly she could only assume it was muscle memory from the days when she must have unbuttoned his shirt before working for her. In moments she had it undone and was pulling it apart and tugging the sleeves down his arms.

Tonino pressed Orla flat back on the bed and gritted his teeth to stifle the feelings threatening to overpower him.

Her hands reached out and touched him… everywhere. His chest, his stomach, his back, scorching his skin and firing his veins. He buried his face into her neck and ran his hands over the slender body he still remembered every inch of.

Just the taste of Orla's kisses was enough to fuel him as no other could.

No wonder the few relationships he'd had since she'd disappeared from his life had ended with barely a whimper. No woman had stood a chance after he'd tasted Orla. She had stayed with him, every minute of every hour, a spectre in the corner of his eye by day and a ghost haunting his dreams by night.

She had taken possession of his heart, slipping in without him realising until it was too late, and he'd lost her.

He had her back now, he thought savagely, and he would never let her go again.

Dragging a hand up a smooth thigh, her dress rising as he went, he pressed his hand over the core of her womanhood.

She moaned into his mouth and tilted her pelvis so it pressed back against his hand, crushing herself against his naked chest. He wanted to feel her naked against him. He wanted to touch the soft skin, to kiss the pert breasts; to kiss every inch of her body, discover the changes pregnancy had wrought on it and get to know it all over again.

Together they dispatched her knickers then he covered her sweet mouth again and, sliding a hand between her legs, he found her wet and writhing for him. Her nub was already swollen, and she moaned loudly when he pressed a finger to it and then dipped down to slide a finger inside her.

Mouths fused together, he captured the hem of her dress and shifted it to her waist, but suddenly found himself unable to move it any higher for Orla had clamped her arms to her sides, preventing him from moving the dress another inch.

'Leave it on,' she whispered into his mouth before darting her tongue back inside the coffee-tasting depths and wrapping her arms back around his waist.

Orla wanted this with a desperation she'd never known before. She wanted to feel everything she'd felt during the conception of their child, a memory that still hadn't taken its full shape, and she knew that the moment he saw her unclothed, the moment would be ruined. She would be ashamed. He would be disgusted. He would ask questions. The moment would be lost.

The feelings erupting through her were too heady, too sensuous, too *everything* for it to be lost.

Guiding his hand back to the place it had been giving her such pleasure, she reached down for the button of his chinos and undid it, then pulled the zip down with an expert precision that came, again, from muscle memory.

She had done all this before and, while she still

didn't remember it, she knew she desperately wanted to do it again. With Tonino. Only Tonino.

She tugged the chinos and underwear down his hips then, with a flexibility she'd never dreamt she possessed, bent her knees and lifted her legs until her toes reached his clothing and she tugged them down with her feet.

Then their mouths were fused together once more and his hand was replaced by something much harder, something long and thick and…

In one long thrust he was inside her. The pleasure was immediate and shockingly powerful.

Orla's moan turned into a sigh as she adjusted to the huge weight filling her and welcomed the sensations that suddenly felt so familiar.

Her body knew exactly what it wanted, and she closed her eyes and let it guide her. One hand buried itself in Tonino's hair, the other grabbed hold of a buttock and drove him deeper and harder inside her as they rocked together with unintelligible whispers and moans.

She reached her peak quickly. All the sensations infusing her fused together into a tight ball that exploded in a rolling crescendo that filled every cell in her body with the most glorious pleasure. No sooner had she welcomed the headiness of her orgasm than Tonino's groans deepened and his thrusts hardened and quickened until he gave a long cry and collapsed on her.

For the longest, dreamiest time, Tonino's weight was spread deliciously on her, his face buried in her neck. She burrowed her fingers in his thick hair and turned her cheek to press her mouth to the top of his head. He kissed her neck then muttered something and withdrew from her. Keeping hold of her, he rolled onto his back, taking her with him so her head rested on his chest.

Slowly the dreamy sensations subsided and the passion that had taken them both in its grip evaporated until all that was left was an ache in her heart and a throb between her legs that felt both new and familiar.

It would be so easy to fall asleep like this. The room was in darkness—there hadn't been the time or thought to switch a light on—the only illumination coming from the starry skies filtering through the windows.

She waited until Tonino's breathing became deep and rhythmic before disentangling herself from his hold.

Sitting up carefully so as not to disturb him, she smiled sadly to see his feet were still on the floor. Not wanting him to get cold, she untangled the bedsheets and folded them over him as much as she could.

Then she slipped off the bed, snatched up her discarded underwear and padded quietly to the door.

She had just put her left foot over the threshold when a rich, deep voice that contained not an ounce of sleepiness caught her short.

'Running away again, *dolcezza*?'

CHAPTER ELEVEN

ORLA WINCED. SHE'D been too hasty in her escape. She should have left it a few minutes longer to ensure Tonino was deep in sleep.

Ashamed at being caught fleeing like an escaped bank robber, she counted to three before turning to face him.

His bedside light switched on and she found herself staring at Tonino's gorgeous yet inscrutable face. 'You don't have to leave.'

She tucked a strand of hair behind an ear then tugged at her dress. 'I can't sleep in this.'

There was a moment of loaded silence before Tonino jumped to his feet. 'Wait there,' he ordered as he opened a door and disappeared behind it. He came back out moments later carrying an item of clothing.

Stalking over to her, he pressed it into her hands. 'Take this. Change in my bathroom. If you look in the cabinet beneath the sink you will find a spare toothbrush. It's never been used.

You are welcome to shower. There are fresh towels. Help yourself to anything you need.'

'I have stuff in my...'

'You are sleeping with me. End of subject. Now, unless you want me to remove your dress and expose the scars you are too frightened to let me see, I suggest you go use the bathroom.'

Something deep inside her withered painfully.

'I called Aislin,' he explained into the loaded silence.

'What?'

He sighed. 'Go and sort yourself out, Orla. I'll explain when you're ready.'

Defeated, afraid she could cry, which she absolutely did not want to do in front of Tonino, she hugged the clothing to her chest and locked herself in his luxury bathroom.

Suddenly desperate to wash the shamed feeling off her skin, she double-checked the door couldn't be unlocked from the bedroom and shed her dress.

Closing her eyes, she welcomed the rush of hot water that stung her skin and turned her face up to it.

Was this how she'd felt the first time they'd made love? Ashamed of herself?

She'd never dreamed she was capable of such wanton, lusty behaviour. Women like her just did not behave in that way. That was for women like her mother, women who embraced chaos, women who didn't care who they hurt or what others thought of them.

Orla did care. She cared deeply. Her pregnancy had shamed her more than any walk of shame the evil authorities had made women perform in medieval times. It wasn't that she'd been unmarried—her grandmother's old-fashioned views hadn't soaked into her *that* much—but that she had given her virginity to a man she'd barely known who she'd then learned she hadn't known at all. All her life she'd believed she would wait for the mythical perfect man from the realms of fairy tales to appear before giving her heart and her body, not a man she'd known barely two days.

That she still wanted Tonino as much as she had then, that one touch of his hand in her hair made her want to rip his clothes off... It mortified her. It terrified her how easily she lost possession of herself for him.

Only when she feared she was using the whole of Sicily's water supply did she switch the shower off and reach for a huge, fluffy towel neatly laid on the heated towelling rail.

She found an unused toothbrush exactly where he'd said and brushed her teeth vigorously, as if she could brush away the demons that plagued her as well as any dirt clinging to her teeth.

And then she shook out the white item of clothing Tonino had given her and felt a tear in her heart.

It was one of his shirts.

Before slipping it over her head she buried her nose in it and inhaled the faint trace of his cologne amidst the laundry soap.

When she finally found the courage to leave his bathroom and face him, she took three large breaths and unlocked the door.

He was sitting up in bed, the sheets covering him to his waist. He was not on his phone or watching television or reading. He was simply waiting for her.

'Better?' he asked sardonically.

Her heart thudded painfully, and she blinked away the wet burn in the backs of her eyes as she nodded.

He patted the space beside him. It was a command, not an invitation.

Climbing onto the bed gingerly, she sat beside him, making sure not to sit close enough that their bodies accidentally touched.

Tonino, however, was not disposed to have her beside him but apart, and, with a glare, he hooked an arm around her waist and pulled her against him.

'Stop fighting me,' he murmured, dropping a kiss onto the top of her head.

'I'm not,' she lied even as she wriggled to free herself from his tight hold.

'Relax, *dolcezza*. I'm not going to rip the shirt off you.'

His chest hair brushed against her cheek. The musky scent of his skin skipped down her airwaves and filtered into her veins and somehow pushed much of the angst inside her out.

A pang rent through her heart.

Being held in his arms like this…

It felt right. It had always felt right.

With a sigh she placed her hand flat on the plane of his stomach and pressed a kiss to the warm skin even as she screwed her eyes tightly together to stop the gathering tears from escaping.

'When did you speak to Aislin?' she asked quietly when she could speak without choking.

'Earlier, when you were getting ready for dinner.'

'Why?'

He smoothed her hair with his hand. 'Because you have been hiding things from me.'

'I haven't hidden anything. Not since we met at the wedding and the missing memories came back. I've been upfront about Finn—'

'I'm not talking about Finn. I'm talking about *you*.' He brushed a finger down her face and tilted her chin up so she was forced to meet his stare. 'Getting information about the long-term effects the accident had on you has been like drawing blood from a stone. You seem to operate on a need-to-know basis, and I think I know why—you're afraid that I will use your injuries as a weapon against you to gain custody of Finn.'

Tonino's instincts were terrifying in their accuracy.

'I know you suffered much more than a head injury,' he continued, his thumb still resting gently under her chin. 'You were partially paralysed and needed three major operations to help you walk and regain your motor functions. You spent six months in hospital and a further year in a rehabilitation centre. Your muscles are still weak and prone to spasm. You regularly sleep ten hours a night because your brain has to work twice as hard as everyone else's to perform simple tasks so you lose your energy quickly. You suffer from debilitating headaches. One of the reasons you both waited six months after your father died before Aislin came to Sicily to fight for your share of his estate was because you were too weak to be left in sole charge of Finn. Have I missed anything?'

Tonino deliberately kept his voice light as he relayed the list of damage inflicted on Orla's beautiful body. He could have continued, could have mentioned the broken ribs and broken arm, but the solitary tear that trickled down her cheek as she shook her head in answer let him know he'd said enough.

He'd called Dante because it had become blindingly obvious that Orla was masking the severity of her own condition. It had been a gradual reckoning until it had reached the point where he noticed it in her every action. Just the way she concentrated when carrying a cup was a big giveaway. He'd had to convince Dante that his intentions in seeking this information were honourable before he'd been put through to Aislin, who'd relayed all the details to him in what had made painful listening.

Orla put a brave face on but she still suffered the effects from it. She might always suffer them.

'You need to learn to trust me.' Tonino bent his head and brushed a soft kiss to her trembling lips. 'I will *never* take Finn from you. You do not have to hide things from me. I want to help you.'

She blinked rapidly and swallowed before whispering, 'I find it hard to trust people.'

He shifted his legs forward and lay down, taking Orla with him, then rolled over so he lay on top of her.

Placing his elbows either side of her head,

he stared into her eyes. 'You need to try. I am not your enemy. I am not going to take our son from you because your injuries mean you can be clumsy and that you need more sleep than me. And I'm not going to stop wanting you because of some scars.'

Her throat moved as she bit into her bottom lip.

Placing a hand on her thigh, he parted her legs and rested his hips between them. 'Do you feel that?' he murmured.

Her eyes widened as his arousal pressed against her and she gave a short, breathless nod.

'No one turns me on the way you do. No one.' Bending his head, he kissed her plump mouth while running a hand down the side of her body then back up to cover her breast. He could feel its softness more easily through the shirt than he could through the thicker material of her dress and bra but he wanted to feel it bare against his hand and feel the nipple pucker in his mouth.

'I will never force you to do anything you don't want,' he whispered as he drove his arousal inside her, savouring the way her neck arched and the softest moan flew from her mouth. He pulled back to the tip then thrust in harder. 'All I want is to give you pleasure.'

Maybe if he showed her all the pleasure they were capable of creating together, the Orla who had given herself to him without reservation four years ago would come back to him.

When Orla opened her eyes the room was bright with daylight. The space beside her on Tonino's bed was empty.

She sat upright, looking for something to tell the time with.

Padding out of the bedroom, she went to Finn's room and found it empty. The nurse's room was empty too.

In her own room she donned some underwear, shrugged her robe on and set off looking for everyone.

She ignored the chiding voice in her head that told her she was being sentimental keeping Tonino's shirt on.

After a search that took far longer than expected, she found her son and his father in Tonino's office. Tonino was reading something on his desktop, Finn sat on the floor building something only he could recognise with his blocks.

They both turned to her when she walked in. 'Mummy!'

She sank to her knees and scooped her son into her arms, then waited a moment for her heart rate to lower to something resembling normality before turning her gaze to Tonino.

Her heart rate accelerated. Images of everything they'd shared the night before flashed in vivid colour before her eyes.

From the knowing smile playing on Tonino's firm mouth, he was having the exact same recollection.

'What time is it?' she asked.

He looked at his watch. 'Eleven.'

She raised her brow in dismay. 'That late? You should have woken me.'

'You needed the sleep, *dolcezza*.' And then he winked, making her cheeks turn into a furnace all over again. 'If you go and get ready, I've promised Finn a swim in the pool.'

The next day, after a couple of hours spent building sandcastles on Tonino's private stretch of beach and eating the picnic lunch made for them by his chef, Finn fell asleep. Removing the sandwich half hanging from his mouth and making sure the parasol shaded his delicate skin, Orla covered him from shoulder to toe with a thin sheet for good measure, then stretched her legs out and lifted her face to the sun's rays.

'You look happy,' Tonino observed, cold bottle of beer in hand.

She nodded, glad she had her shades on so he couldn't see what lay behind them. Sometimes it felt as if he only had to look into her eyes, and he could read everything in her head.

This was the second day in a row she'd woken in Tonino's bed, replete by a night of lovemaking. Her promises to self that she would sleep in her own bed had been broken pretty much the moment she'd made them.

Deny herself the opportunity of making love to Tonino again? She was no masochist.

Or was she?

Was the heady pleasure she found in his bed worth the inevitable heartache heading her way?

'Finn's happy here too,' he added into the silence before helping himself to a chunk of honeydew melon.

She looked at their sleeping son and could only agree.

'Have you thought any more about us marrying?' he asked.

Her answer was automatic. 'No.' She shook her head for good measure, her loose ponytail whipping with a crack.

He exhaled slowly. 'What is stopping you from saying yes?'

'Everything that stopped me when you first suggested it. Marriage is a terrible idea.'

An edge crept into his voice. 'Why?'

Orla felt an edge form inside her too, defensive spikes lifting beneath her skin. 'Because it wouldn't mean what it should mean. You wouldn't even be thinking it if it weren't for

Finn. I mean, come on, four years ago you pretended to be someone else and, while I believe you about Sophia, it doesn't change that you did lie about your identity, and the only reason I can see for you doing that is because you never took me seriously from the start. I was so far removed from what you considered suitable wife material that you didn't need bother tell me the truth.'

A long pause of silence opened up between them, broken when Tonino took a swig of his beer.

'Thoughts of your *suitability*...' he delivered the word with a curled lip '...didn't cross my mind. When we first met my only thoughts were of bedding you. You didn't know me. You had no preconceptions. You just wanted me. And that felt great.'

He turned his head to face her. Even with both their eyes masked by sunglasses, his gaze penetrated her flesh and set her heart racing.

She remembered her own instinctive reaction when she'd learned the wealth, connections and power Tonino and his family had. It had frightened her. For many other women, it would have attracted them.

His voice lowered. 'But then you got under my skin and I knew I had to tell you the truth. The mistake I made was to fly to Tuscany before telling you because Sophia got to you first and fed you all those lies.'

'No, the mistake you made was not telling me the truth to begin with.' She shook her head to clear it from the effects of Tonino's seductive voice. He had a voice that could recite the worst kind of poetry and make it sound like a masterpiece. 'You were playing with me. I was just a joke to you, some naïve Irish girl you could play make-believe with.'

He downed the last of his beer. 'Maybe it started like that,' he admitted, 'but that is not how it finished. I fell for you, *dolcezza*, harder than I had ever fallen for anyone, and you ran away rather than confront me and allow me to defend myself. You believed Sophia's lies.'

'She was very convincing.' She rubbed her cheeks, feeling wretched. He was right. She hadn't given him the chance to defend himself from Sophia's lies.

'Sophia is a superb actress.'

'I think her hatred of me is genuine.'

'What hatred? What makes you say that?'

'Did you not see the dirty looks she kept throwing me at Aislin and Dante's wedding?'

'All I remember from that wedding is feeling sucker-punched by your reappearance in my life.'

'She looked like she wanted to throttle me.'

'Don't take it personally. She looks at everyone like that.' Tonino popped the cap off another beer, removed his sunglasses and looked at her squarely. 'I've known Sophia all my life. She's a bitch, yes, but she would never hurt you. She's married now and has a child of her own.'

'Oh.' She gave a shaky laugh. 'I suppose I imagined she'd spent the past four years making effigies of me.'

'Put your fears to rest. She is a professional grudge holder, but her violence is only verbal.'

'But why the grudge? If you didn't cheat on her with me, why does she hate me?'

'Because she knows I ended our engagement for you.'

'What...?' Until Orla had lost her memories, Sophia's pain and her unwitting contribution towards it had plagued her. She'd hoped she could put her guilt to bed but now Tonino was saying the ending of his engagement *had* been about her? 'You ended your engagement for *me*?'

Long moments passed before his nostrils flared. 'It wasn't strictly about you. It was about my desire for you. It was a desire no man who is bound to one person should feel for another.'

'I might be Irish but that's a riddle too far, even for me.'

He laughed but it contained a bitter tinge.

'The truth is, Sophia and I should never have got engaged.'

'Then why did you?'

'It was something our families always hoped for. Our mothers have been friends since they were babies. It was a running joke between them from when *we* were babies that Sophia and I would marry and as I neared thirty and felt the urge to settle down, marrying her made sense. On paper we were perfect for each other. You see, *dolcezza*, when you're rich you have to think of marriage in terms of reputation and with an eye to the future. My personal reputation is of little concern to me, but my parents' reputations matter greatly to them. Marriage to a Messina, a family as old and as noble as the Valentes, could only enhance that. And vice versa.'

'How did they take the ending of the engagement?'

She caught the flash of bitterness on his features.

'Not well?' she guessed.

'No,' he agreed shortly.

'I suppose that was understandable.'

His features sharpened. 'Understandable?'

Feeling she was dipping her toe in water infested by sharks that no one had told her about, she said tentatively, 'If they were such good friends with Sophia's parents, it must have been embarrassing for them.'

His jaw clenched. 'They weren't embarrassed. They were furious that I'd ruined their dream. They accused me of disloyalty. Can you believe that?' He ran an angry hand through his hair and shook his head. 'I knew they wouldn't be happy about it, but I never expected my mother to come *this* close to slapping my face or for my father to threaten to disinherit me if I didn't change my mind.' He made a distinctive snorting sound. 'As if I cared about his money. I was already worth far more than him.'

Orla, thinking of all the times her grandmother had threatened to cut her mother off without a penny without actually going through with it—after her death, her mother had shared the small inheritance with her siblings—said softly, 'And how are things between you now? I assume they must be better if we're taking Finn to their party.'

He made the snorting sound again.

Dismissive. That was what it sounded like.

'I will never forgive them for putting their reputations and pride above my happiness but they're still my parents. We're still a family and nothing can change that.'

'*Did* they disinherit you?'

Her question caused him to pause then give a low chuckle. 'Not as far as I know.'

'The threat was made in anger?'

He didn't answer.

Despite the seriousness of the discussion, a bubble of laughter rose up Orla's throat. 'You are *so* your father's son.'

'What do you mean?'

'When you get angry you make threats you don't mean. Like your threats of taking custody of Finn… I wonder if he'll inherit the Valente temper,' she added musingly.

Tonino stared at her, part in disbelief. Was she taking his parents' side? Surely not? If it had been one short argument he would get her point but he'd lived with their hot fury for months, a period when his mother could hardly bring herself to look at him. The first big argument had come the evening he'd ended it. He'd done the right thing by telling them personally and immediately.

He'd found solace from their fury in Orla's arms. He'd turned his phone off and cloistered her in his oldest apartment. Those magical days together had pushed the mess he'd created far from his mind. Unfortunately it had given his parents the time and space to build everything up so when he'd next seen them, they'd been ready to unload their venom at him. Reeling at their selfishness, reeling from Orla's disappearance, he'd unloaded right back at them.

'There are some lines that should never be crossed,' he said shortly. 'And now that I'm a father it makes their reaction even more unforgivable.'

'Oh, come *on*.' Her shades masked her eyes, but he could swear he heard her eyes roll. 'They're only human. Life's too short to hold on to grudges.'

'Can you forgive *your* mother?'

'That's completely different. She was always a useless parent.' And then she surprised him completely by climbing onto his lap and straddling him. She wrapped her arms around his neck and sighed. 'Remember, to err is human, to forgive divine.'

'When are you going to forgive me?'

'I'm working on it.' And then she kissed him with such tenderness that if Finn hadn't been sleeping beside them, he would have ripped both their shorts off and taken her there and then.

CHAPTER TWELVE

LATER THAT NIGHT, dressed only in Tonino's shirt, which she'd adopted as her own, and replete in his arms, Orla made circles around his nipples. 'Can I ask you something?'

He answered sleepily, 'Anything.'

'Did you have any feelings for Sophia?'

She had no idea how she was going to feel whatever answer he gave, but it was a question that had been bugging her since their earlier trip to the beach. It took such a long time for him to answer that she thought he'd fallen asleep, but then a hand burrowed into her hair.

'I was attracted to her—Sophia is a beautiful woman—but that's as far as my feelings towards her went.' He sighed. 'The chemistry was not there. Not for me. I assumed familiarity would breed desire but I was wrong—all it bred was contempt. We'd been childhood friends but the more I got to know the grown-up Sophia, the less I liked her.' He twirled a lock of her hair around his finger, his voice dropping to a murmur. 'But it was only when a beautiful Irishwoman walked into my hotel that I knew I had to end the engagement.'

Her heart skipped.

Tonino kissed her head and tightened his hold around her. 'You, *dolcezza*, were the most beautiful woman I had ever set eyes on. I spent the day organising the refurbishment of your room when I should have been in meetings with lawyers and accountants.'

He felt the heavy beats of her heart pressing against his stomach. He felt the stirrings of arousal.

'I could not stop myself from fantasising about you. I fantasised about stripping you naked and making love to you.' The stirrings grew stronger. 'They were fantasies that told me I had to end things with Sophia—how could I marry her when I felt such intense desire for someone else? I did the honourable thing and ended the engagement immediately. I did not ask you out until after I'd spoken to her. When we made love, I was a free man.' Moving smoothly, he manoeuvred her onto her back and covered her body with his. 'And I am still a free man. Marry me and you will have me for ever.'

She stared up at him, her eyes like dazed orbs. Cupping her cheeks, he pressed his nose to hers. 'You, *dolcezza*, are still the most beautiful woman I have ever seen. There is no one like you in this world. I have never wanted anyone the way I want you. You are under my skin and in my blood. I want you there for ever.'

And then he kissed her.

Orla, hypnotised as much by his voice as his words, sank into the firmness of his mouth with a sigh, a throb deep inside her already singing its head off in anticipation.

He'd never wanted anyone the way he wanted her?

Well, she'd never wanted anyone *but* him...

'Finn can have a good life here,' he murmured as he kissed her neck. 'He will have family, cousins to play with, sunshine, ripe fruits... everything he needs to thrive.' He captured a nipple over the cotton of the shirt covering her body and sucked it greedily. 'If you won't marry me, live with me. Move in...' He moved lower, kissing her shirt-covered belly, taking hold of her thighs and gently spreading them. 'You will be close to Aislin and Dante.' He moved even lower and gently raised her bottom. 'I know how much you miss them.'

'You...don't...play...fair,' she groaned, stickily wet and aching for him.

'I play to win.' He pressed his thumb to her swollen clitoris.

She moaned and grabbed hold of the pillow.

'Tell me this doesn't feel like winning to you too.' And then he replaced his thumb with his tongue and any semblance of coherent thought vanished as Orla was suffused in intense, hedonistic pleasure.

'We'll stay until the party. Save Finn having to do all that travelling.'

Orla's whispered words cut through the sleep pulling Tonino under.

He kissed her shoulder and murmured, 'If you move in he won't have to do any travelling between our countries.'

'I know.'

'Think about it. For Finn's sake.'

And, as Tonino finally fell into the oblivion of sleep, his last conscious thought was that it would be for his own sake too.

The next ten days passed with nothing more said about marriage or them living together. At first Orla had been glad of the reprieve but the longer time passed, the less she trusted it. Tonino was quite capable of bamboozling her with the subject when she least suspected it. She was supposed to be returning to Ireland tomorrow and was still no closer to making a decision.

The problem was, she admitted to herself, she

was torn between her head and her heart. Her heart wanted Finn to have all the advantages living in Sicily would give him. Her head, however, kept pointing out that Tonino only wanted her for Finn. The sex between them was just a bonus—a free leg-over, as her grandmother would have primly called it.

But not for Orla. For Orla, the sex they shared… In the depths of her consciousness, she called it making love.

To make things worse, she missed him when he wasn't there.

He'd been with her and Finn all the time during their first week in his home but then, during their second week, he'd had to work. Work for Tonino consisted of attending important meetings and travelling around Europe on business. At least, that was how it looked to Orla.

There was something incredibly sexy about watching this hunk of a man dress for work, tucking a crisply ironed shirt into his tailored trousers, doing the buttons of the waistcoat, fixing his cufflinks into place, tying the laces of his handmade shoes… The urge to leap out from under the bedsheets and pounce on him would hit her so hard that she would clench her fists and force her mind to think of non-sexy things, like dirty laundry.

How was it possible to ache for someone so

badly? And how was it possible to miss someone so much that she kept her phone close at all
times, hurrying to answer it whenever he called.
Which was often.

He was considerate too. The nights he arrived
back so late that she'd already fallen asleep, he
would slip into bed and do nothing more than
wrap his arms around her. He didn't wake her
for sex. He let her sleep, saving their lovemaking for the morning.

Then yesterday he'd arrived back at the chateau at lunchtime declaring his working week
over, and she'd had to fight her legs again not
to pounce on him with glee at having him back.
Finn had been thrilled to see him too. He'd been
so overjoyed to see his father that Orla's happiness had dimmed and she'd found herself torn
into pieces with contradictory emotions that
shamed her.

She was ashamed too that the moment he'd
left for work on Monday, she'd got straight onto
the phone and video-called Aislin for advice,
shamed that she called herself an adult when
she couldn't make a decision and shamed to be
disturbing her sister's honeymoon.

Aislin had listened carefully to Orla's woe
then her face had lit up. 'I *knew* it! He's nuts
about you.' She'd burst into peals of laughter.

'If he still wants you after I made that threat to him, he's nuts at the least.'

'Are you drunk?'

'On happiness!'

'He isn't nuts about me. He wants Finn. I'm just the mother of his son.'

Aislin had rolled her eyes. 'You really need to get out more if you believe that. Look, missus, don't rush into any hasty decisions but, from my perspective, it would be grand if you moved to Sicily. I miss you and Finn.'

'You're having your own baby.'

'And my baby will want his aunty and cousin close by. I'm not telling you to marry him or even live with him, but if you could bring yourself to live in Sicily then we'll all be happy.'

'Why does it have to be *my* life that's uprooted?'

'Because you don't have a life.'

That was a fact Orla could not argue with.

She'd had a life once. A long time ago. When she'd first met Tonino she'd been excited to embrace the newest chapter of it by starting her dream job. The pregnancy had seen the future she'd worked so hard for slip through her fingers. The accident and its aftermath meant it was unlikely she would ever work again. Even if she could, she didn't think she'd be able to leave Finn. And if she couldn't contemplate leaving him for a few hours a day for a job, then how would she cope letting him visit his father for weeks at a time?

Everything pointed to her agreeing to live with Tonino. Or she could do as Aislin suggested and just move to Sicily independently, but that would only cause additional issues.

Marriage was out of the question. Marriage was a commitment that should only be entered between two people who meant their vows. Her mother had been shamed into marrying Aislin's father because her grandmother couldn't bear the shame of her daughter having a second illegitimate child by a second man. The marriage had been a disaster and ended after two years.

Deep down was the painful peripheral wish that Tonino's proposal meant more than a means to having their son living under his roof, but she would not let her mind go there.

She could smack her head with frustration at the choice she had to make.

Time was running out.

Tonino was expecting an answer that evening, when they returned from his parents' party.

Keen to make a good first impression with his family for Finn's sake, Orla left Finn with Tonino while she got ready. She went through her wardrobe half a dozen times before selecting a dark blue dress with chunky crystals running the length of its high neckline. It also had the requisite long sleeves and its mid-thigh-length skirt had a slight swing to it. All the sun she'd been living with these past few weeks had given her legs some colour, which was a nice bonus.

Before dressing, she put on matching lacy blue underwear then applied the topical lotion to her itching scars. The scars on her back were itching too and she slipped her robe on and, lotion in hand, knocked on the duty nurse's bedroom door.

The nurse was halfway through administering it, with her usual lecture of letting the lotion sink into the skin before Orla dressed, when there was a loud rap on the door adjoining the nurse's room with Finn's. To Orla's horror, the door couldn't have been shut properly for the weight of the knock caused it to swing open.

Tonino stood in the doorway, his hand raised. When he saw the nurse, he immediately burst into a flurry of Sicilian that died on his tongue when he caught sight of a frozen Orla.

The nurse seemed to sense her horror and immediately stepped between them, acting as a barrier so Orla could wrap the robe back around herself and hurry out of the room, cheeks flaming with humiliation.

* * *

Tonino wished he'd chosen to drive. It would have given him something to concentrate on.

Instead he sat in the back of his limousine trying to forget that his lover had frozen in horror at him seeing her in her underwear.

It was the closest he'd come to seeing her naked in four years. She'd run from the room like a frightened rabbit.

So much for the progress he'd believed they were making.

Things had been good between them. For the first time in for ever he'd shunned staying at his hotels during his business travels, keen to return home to his son and his son's mother.

Her frightened rabbit eyes had brought him crashing back to earth. There had been such fear in them that he'd barely registered her lack of clothing or looked at the scars she kept hidden from him.

Orla did not trust him.

She would allow the nurse to see her scars but allowing the man she shared a bed with every night to see them? Not a chance. They made love constantly, but she always kept her top half clothed.

'Do your parents know Finn was conceived with the woman you ended things with Sophia for?' she asked shortly after Finn fell asleep to the motion of the car.

He paused a moment before answering. Now was not the time for an argument. Not when they had to deal with his family. He needed to keep his anger contained. 'I don't know. I haven't discussed it with them.'

'What about when you met with your mother yesterday?' After his early return home from work, he'd taken Finn out to meet his mother. It was the first time they had done anything without Orla and it had felt strange not having her with them.

'It wasn't mentioned.' Their meeting in a beach café had been the warmest exchange between them in four years. His mother had taken one look at Finn's huge brown eyes and visibly softened. Her unabashed delight at meeting her grandson had almost—almost—made Tonino soften too.

Orla's words about forgiveness had played in his head. At first, he'd dismissed it out of hand but her comment about him having his father's temper had played on his mind too. There was truth in it.

It had taken months for things to settle down into the semblance of normality between Tonino and his parents but, though they all went through the motions of being a family, things had never been the same. There had always been a frisson of ice between them. Embraces were perfunctory. Kisses did not connect with cheeks. For that, he had always blamed them.

Maybe it was time to look at his own actions and put himself in their shoes. He'd caused the end of a great friendship and, like it or not, he'd brought shame on them both.

He despised the selfishness of their reaction but for the first time he accepted Orla's observation that it had been provoked by anger; a rush of blood to the head. When he'd effectively gone into hiding by practically chaining Orla to his bed and disconnecting his doorbell and turning his phone off, it had given his parents time for their fury to percolate. When he'd re-emerged, all their fury had blasted at him like a solar flare.

Shattered from Orla's desertion, he'd fired back at them. All the pain her leaving had caused him, he'd thrown onto his parents' shoulders.

He'd been an idiot, he acknowledged grimly.

'Your family can do rudimentary maths.' Orla's lyrical brogue cut through his thoughts. 'They will know Finn's conception coincided with your engagement ending. What if they take against him for it?'

'Why on earth would they do that?' he asked, astonished she would even suggest such a thing.

She stared out of the window. 'People have a habit of blaming children for the sins of their parents.'

'Are you talking generally or from experience?'

'Both. Dante was tarnished because of our father's gambling problem and womanising. Those things were nothing to do with him and completely beyond his control, yet he almost lost a business deal because of it.'

'And you? Have you had something similar happen?'

Turning her head to look at him, she said simply, 'My conception is something that's hung over me my entire life.'

Unsure if she was joking—*hoping* she was joking—he responded with a bemused, 'It's the twenty-first century.'

'That doesn't mean everyone has twenty-first-century ideals, especially in the village I grew up in. I was a walking reminder of my mother's shame—or should I say, her lack of it?' She gave a laugh that contained no humour at all.

'*Should* she have felt shame?' he asked curiously. He despised Orla's mother for abandoning her daughters and grandson when they needed her most, but it wasn't like Orla to be judgemental. 'She wasn't the married party in the affair. Salvatore was.'

'I don't know.' She shrugged in a helpless fashion and sighed. 'I used to know. It was all very cut and dried when I was a child. I had the mummy who went on holiday to Sicily and came home knocked up by a married man. Everyone knew I was the product of an affair.' She sighed again and rested her head back. 'I get it now, why you didn't tell me who you really were. It was similar to my reasons for not telling you I was Salvatore Moncada's illegitimate daughter. I didn't want you having any preconceived thoughts about me or for you to think I was easy like my mother.'

'I would never think that.'

'I know that now.' She caught his eye and smiled sadly. 'I'm really glad your mother has been so kind to Finn and that she wants a relationship with him, and I know I'm being selfish but I can't help worry about how your family will feel about me. I mean, you said the other week that reputation matters to them. Do they know who I am?'

'Yes. Believe it or not, the fact you're Dante Moncada's sister and half Sicilian works in your favour.'

Her nose wrinkled. *Really?'*

He gave a short burst of humourless laughter. 'Really. You have the required pedigree.'

'I'm not a dog,' she said, visibly affronted.

'Obviously,' he answered wryly. 'But trust me on this; you have nothing to worry about with my family. They've been so worried that I'll never settle down and produce grandchildren that they wouldn't care if you were part of the *Cosa Nostra*.'

'Charming!' she said with a roll of her eyes. 'Is that why you never settled down after Sophia? To punish your family for not supporting you?'

Her question threw him.

Had he been punishing them? Punishing his parents for destroying his trust in the unconditional love he'd always taken for granted by not attempting to understand his feelings?

Didn't he bear some responsibility for it too?

He remembered seeing his father's face go red with fury when he'd broken the news and feeling his own anger rise in turn. They'd been like a pair of rutting bulls.

Whatever the truth, when his parents' villa came into view, for the first time in four years the rancid curdle of acid he usually felt to be there was absent.

CHAPTER THIRTEEN

ORLA COULD NOT suck enough air into her lungs to kill the terror clawing at her as they approached Tonino's parents. Never minding Finn's conception and the end of the future marriage with their dream daughter-in-law, they were both powerful people. What on earth were they going to think of a little minnow like her?

The terror only evaporated when Angelica and Paolo Valente both pulled her into tight embraces and smothered her cheeks with kisses.

Who needed to speak a common language when body language so perfectly conveyed meaning? she thought dazedly.

The language barrier was much less a problem when Tonino introduced her to his brother and sister-in-law, both of whom spoke good English and embraced her with equal vigour.

However, the language barrier was the last thing to cross her mind when she was introduced to his sister. Orla recognised her instantly.

Giulia Valente, barely a month after giving birth to her third child, looked as young and beautiful as she'd done in the photograph Orla had seen of her and Tonino in the Internet search that had caused Finn to kick her so memorably hard.

What had happened after she'd seen that photo? She *knew* it was important but, as had been the case for over three years, trying to force a memory only pushed it further into the shadows.

With whispered thanks, she accepted a glass of lemonade made from the fruit of the Valentes' lemon grove and slowly relaxed. Tonino's family were wonderfully hospitable. Here, at the customary party Angelica and Paolo always threw to celebrate the birth of a new grandchild— something it seemed, as the entire family had assured her, would be done for Finn too—was all Tonino's extended family, all his aunts, uncles, grandparents, the multitude of first and second cousins… It sent a pang through her to witness the closeness they all shared. Orla's family was of comparable size, but they had little day-to-day involvement in each other's lives. Not a single one of them had visited her or Finn in hospital or offered to help share the load Aislin had taken in caring for them. This Sicilian lot, she thought, would pack the hospital out if one of their own fell ill.

A silent tour of the villa led by Angelica herself, who held Orla's hand throughout, took her breath away. It matched Tonino's for size and elegance but with added homeliness.

If she moved in with Tonino, she would have to have a chat with him about feminising the chateau a little.

If...?

Surely the operative word now was 'when'. Because as the day went on, her indecision evaporated just as her terror had done.

She had to put her own feelings to one side and think of Finn. Sicily was the best place for him to be raised. Just look at all these people fussing over him! These people were his family and they would never let him down or abandon him. If she moved in with Tonino they would have Aislin living close to them, and Dante too.

She wouldn't be alone as she was in Ireland.

After the tour, she sat with Angelica on a garden bench waiting for Tonino to return from giving Finn his own tour of the villa.

As neither woman spoke the other's language, they didn't converse and yet there was something companionable and protective about the way Angelica positioned herself. She had an innate glamour similar to Dante's mother but if she'd had any work on her beautiful features, it was as subtle as subtle could be. She wore her intelligence much more freely.

A shout from the villa made them both get to their feet to see what the commotion was about.

A moment later, one of Tonino's nieces came flying out of the villa and raced straight to Orla, tugging her hand. Orla didn't need to speak Sicilian to know the young girl was begging her to come with her. Distress was its own universal language.

Call it sixth sense, call it mother's intuition, but she knew immediately what was happening and what she would find, and, clinging to the young girl's hand, she ran inside.

Finn was on the floor of the living room, Tonino crouched beside him, a crowd of young children surrounding him. His tiny body was rigid, convulsions racking him.

'Everyone stand back,' she barked, immediately hitting autopilot.

But, of course, they didn't understand her.

A visibly distressed Tonino blinked then barked what she assumed was the same order in Sicilian. The circle around her convulsing child parted, leaving only Tonino.

'You need to stand back too,' Orla ordered. There was no time for pleasantries.

Dark colour stained his clenched features but he did as she asked.

Sinking to her knees, Orla carefully moved Finn onto his side and placed her hand on his tiny head. His arms jerked, his legs thrashed but it was his eyes she always found the most terrifying. They stared wide open but didn't see.

Tonino had never felt so useless in his life. Or as scared. His heart had stuck in his throat the moment he'd seen his son topple from his sitting position on the floor of the living room where Tonino had put him so he could play with his cousins. His body had gone into spasm with the movements Tonino had seen on videos when learning all he could about his son's condition.

The sounds that had come from his son's poor throat...

Those were sounds that would haunt him.

Thank God for Orla.

All she did was sit beside their son and stroke his hair and whisper soothing words, but it acted like magic. There was not one person in that room who didn't feel it too.

Tonino had no idea if Finn heard his mother's voice or saw her face until the convulsions began to subside, but he was as certain as he could be that his son felt her presence even if only on a subconscious level. When his eyes slowly regained their focus, they stayed on Orla; he was clearly frightened but taking every ounce of comfort he could from his mummy.

It struck Tonino that she only knew what to do and could handle it so calmly because she had lived it many times before.

And it struck him too that she had pushed him aside because she didn't trust him to handle the situation and look after their son.

The harsh truth was that Orla would never trust him.

Orla smoothed Finn's bedsheet over him and kissed his forehead. He was already asleep.

Tonino hovered in the doorway, watching, waiting for his turn to kiss their son goodnight.

She waited for him in the corridor.

He shut the door and looked at her with exhausted eyes. 'I need a drink.'

She closed her eyes. 'I think I could do with one too.'

She followed him to the outdoor bar, which overlooked the swimming pool. The terrace area had a canopy overhanging individual round sofas that were perfect for curling up on and she sank into one with a grateful sigh.

Checking the volume of her phone was switched on, she placed it on the sofa's arm. If the nurse had any concerns, she would be able to reach her straight away.

A crystal glass with a small measure of amber liquid in it was thrust at her.

She took it from Tonino's hand with a muttered thank you and had a tiny sip of it. When heat flowed down her throat she was glad she'd stuck to a tiny sip.

'That was the most terrifying thing I have ever seen,' he said bluntly as he sat heavily on the seat across from hers, putting the bottle of liquor on the floor beside his feet while he cradled his full glass.

She smiled ruefully and tucked her legs under her bottom. 'Yes.'

'You didn't trust me to help you.'

'Sorry?'

He breathed heavily through his nose. 'As soon as you reached Finn you took control and pushed everyone out. Including me.'

'No, I didn't,' she denied, confused.

He tipped a third of his drink down his throat and angrily brushed away the residue on his mouth with his thumb. 'You did.'

'If I insulted or hurt you, then I'm sorry.' She shrugged her shoulders helplessly. 'When Finn has these fits, I go into automatic pilot.'

There was the slightest softening in his stance. He ran a hand over his bowed head. 'Does it get easier?'

She shook her head sadly. 'No. You just get better at dealing with it while it's happening. It happens rarely now that he's on the new medication but the first time it happened in front of me, I practically ran around the room banging into the walls in panic.'

He lifted his head to meet her stare. 'When you say the first time it happened in front of you…?'

She sighed and took another tiny sip. 'When the convulsions started, I was still in the rehab centre. Aislin was the one to deal with it. She had to deal with everything about his condition until I was well enough to play my part.'

His dark brown eyes stayed on hers thoughtfully. She thought he was going to say something but he didn't.

With the warmth from the liquor making her feel calmer inside, she decided now was the time to tell him.

'I've been thinking about your suggestion of Finn and I moving in with you,' she said tentatively.

He raised a brow.

'And I think you're right. It would be better for Finn to live here.'

He continued staring at her expressionlessly.

'We'll move in with you…if the offer still stands,' she added when the lack of emotion on his face injected a jolt of ice up her spine.

He took a much larger drink of his liquor. 'Are you prepared to marry me?'

'You already know the answer to that.'

'You still refuse my proposal?'

'Come on, Tonino, it's nothing personal. I just don't want us to marry.'

'Then I decline.'

She uncurled her legs and sat upright. 'What do you mean?'

'I have been thinking too and I have decided it has to be marriage or nothing.'

'What? But why?'

'Because it's the only way I can trust that you're committed to us.'

'Living with you would show that commitment.'

He shook his head violently and downed the last of his drink. 'No, *dolcezza*, all it would show is that you're committed for the next five minutes.'

'You still don't trust me?'

His burst of laughter was loud and bitter. 'Unfortunately I have the opposite problem. I *do* trust you. I know you well enough now that I believe you always intended to tell me about Finn. I know you well enough to say with confidence that your reasons for keeping the pregnancy secret from me were justified—I still think they were wrong, but I believe *you* believed you were doing the right thing.'

'I don't understand what you're saying.'

He unscrewed the bottle and poured himself another full glass. 'I'm saying that you always do what you think is best for Finn. He is your priority.'

'As he should be.'

'Agreed. But not at the cost of tying yourself to a man you don't love or trust. If you loved or trusted me, you would marry me. But you don't so all you're prepared to give is a half-hearted commitment that you can walk away from any time you like.'

'I wouldn't do that.'

'No? You say that when you don't deny you neither love nor trust me?'

'Well, it's hardly as if you love me.'

'Don't I?'

She blinked. 'Do you?'

His gaze held hers before he shook his head grimly and had another drink. 'When we were on the beach last week, you accused me of treating you like a joke four years ago. The truth is, you were the one who treated me like a joke. You treated me like I was nothing.'

Indignant, she snapped, 'I did *not*...'

'Then why did you not give me a chance to defend myself against Sophia's lies? You have never explained that to me.'

She opened her mouth to answer but nothing came out.

Why *hadn't* she confronted him?

'Why did you run?' he asked roughly. 'Why block my number? If you'd cared for me in any way, you would have given me that chance.'

'I ran because I was already an emotional wreck,' she blurted out.

He stared at her grimly. His mouth clamped shut, forcing her to fill the silence.

'The day you went to Tuscany, I went to see my father. I knew he was due back in Sicily that day and I was desperate to finally meet him.' Her eyes filled with tears and she blinked them back. The last thing she needed right then was to cry but the memory had surfaced with painful vividness. She wished it would lock itself back in its box. 'He wouldn't see me. He refused. The dirty little secret had to remain a dirty little secret. And then I got to the hotel and found Sophia waiting for me with evidence that the man I'd been sleeping with was engaged to another woman and I felt *sick* with myself and so ashamed.'

Not a flicker of emotion crossed his stony face. 'Even if Sophia had been telling the truth it wouldn't have been your fault.'

'Maybe not but that's not how it felt. In the space of two hours I'd been rejected by my father and learned the man I was falling in love with was a cheat and a liar. All I could think of was getting out of Sicily and away from the Sicilian men who'd lied and hurt me.'

'So because your father was a womanising coward, you decided I was of the same mould? Without giving me the right to reply, you grabbed the chance to run away, and when you found you were pregnant and discovered the family I come from is powerful, it gave you another excuse to keep your distance for that bit longer, didn't it? You don't trust anyone.'

'I trust you...'

'Do not *lie* to me,' he snarled with such force she jumped. 'The only person you trust is your sister. If you trusted me even a little you wouldn't go to such great lengths to hide from me. You share your body with me every night, you sleep in my arms, yet you think me a shallow misogynist who runs at the first sight of a blemish on a woman's skin.'

'I don't think that about you.'

'Then explain yourself. Tell me why I am not good enough to look at you.'

'It isn't like that,' she beseeched, fighting even harder to stop the tears from falling. 'My scars will disgust you.'

'Your opinion of me is even worse than I thought.'

'*No*, that is *not* what I'm saying. My scars...' She tugged at her hair and tried to verbalise everything racing through her burning brain. 'I remember the woman I was—the woman you remember—and then I look in the mirror and see the woman I've become, and I'm reminded of everything I've lost and everything Finn's lost. That seizure he had today…that was *mild* compared to the ones he used to have. He has suffered every single day of his life and he will never have a normal childhood. I woke up in a hospital unable to move and unable to communicate. I didn't know if the child in my belly was dead or alive. I couldn't hold him until he was a year old and even then Aislin had to help because I was too weak to hold him on my own. I screamed with pain every day for a year and pushed myself harder than I would have believed possible to get home to my child and all I have to show for it now are the scars on my body. My pain is over, but his suffering will never end. I look at my scars and my heart shreds for the suffering our child has to bear, which he will have to bear every day for the rest of his life, and you think I should *flaunt* them to you?'

His jaw throbbed. 'No, *dolcezza*, I do not expect you to flaunt them. I expect you to share them with me as the father of your child who feels terrible guilt that his bit of fun with a beautiful Irishwoman had such tragic consequences.'

Feeling all the emotions inside her leech out, Orla put her glass on the floor and buried her face in her hands. 'You have nothing to feel guilty about. You have only tried to do the right thing since you learned about Finn.'

'I missed the first three years of his life. Those are years I will never get back.'

'I'm sorry.'

'We are both beyond apologies, do you not think? We both feel guilt, but we have to try and accept that it does not solve anything. You have put our child first since the day you learned you carried him. It is time for me to put him first too. I want to be a permanent part of his life, but I see that it is impossible.'

'What are you saying?'

'That you should return to Ireland with him. It's his home. His language. Where he is comfortable and familiar.'

'But…'

'I will still see him. I visit Ireland regularly. And I will have him visit for holidays.'

'That does not sound like the joint custody we spoke of.'

'Joint custody will not work for Finn. He needs stability. *You* are his stability.' Tonino squeezed his eyes shut as he recalled the look in Finn's eyes when he'd come out of the seizure and locked onto Orla's loving stare. Orla was his son's world. He had to accept that.

'Stay here for a few more days to let him recover from the seizure. I will take myself away somewhere.'

'What are you talking about?'

Dragging air into his tightened lungs, he picked up the bottle, got to his feet and took three heavy paces to the bar.

'Tonino...' she said tentatively. 'Are you calling it a day between us?'

He laughed. '*Dio*, you nearly sound upset.'

Four years ago Orla hadn't known of his trappings of wealth and had fallen for him regardless. She'd looked into his heart as no one else had done and fallen for him...but only to a point. The moment doubts had crept in she'd run away like the coward she was. And now, four years on, when she knew perfectly well his wealth, still she looked in the heart of him and decided he wasn't enough. She did not love him. She did not trust him.

He did not believe she would ever trust him. Without trust there could never be love.

'But is that what you're saying?' she persisted. 'You want to call it off because I won't marry you? And you're the one who laughed at me for being old-fashioned?'

'Do not dare use humour to wriggle out of

this,' he snarled, twisting round to face her. 'I have done nothing but my best to accommodate you.'

'For Finn's sake,' she whispered. All the colour had drained from her face.

'And for yours.' He swore loudly and poured himself another drink. 'Everything I have done has been with you in mind too and all you do is resist me. You won't give an inch and you won't trust me, not with your heart, your body or our son's health.'

'That's not fair and it's not true—'

'For the last time, stop *lying*!' He slammed his glass on the bar, spilling amber liquid all over his hand and the bar surface. There was clarity in the spilled liquid that focused the mind and made him take a long breath to find clarity in his thoughts. 'If you can't stop lying to me then at least stop lying to yourself.'

Tonino would not lie to himself any more either. After four years of lies, the truth he had buried deep in his subconscious had risen up as clear as the spilt liquor on his hand.

He had never got over Orla.

He suspected that he'd fallen in love with her four years ago. He'd certainly never forgotten her or got over her, even when he'd carried on with his life and pushed her from his mind. Only in his dreams had she come back to him. Orla was the reason he'd never settled down. It was nothing to do with punishing his parents—it was because there was no room left in his heart for anyone else.

He suspected too that his purchase of the Bally House Hotel in Dublin had been a subconscious effort to put himself on the same soil as her.

And he suspected, too, that if he continued to live under the same roof as her, knowing his love for her would be unrequited for ever, he would drive himself insane.

All these years he'd been waiting for Orla to come back to him and he hadn't even known it.

He'd finally had a taste of life as a family with the woman he loved and the child he worshipped but it wasn't enough for her. *He* wasn't enough for her.

Any ties they'd forged together had been ripped apart.

It was time to say goodbye.

CHAPTER FOURTEEN

ORLA INSPECTED FINN from head to toe, ensuring not a speck of lint or dust marred his miniature tuxedo, then rewarded him with a beaming smile. 'You, young man, look delicious.'

He beamed.

'In fact, if your daddy wasn't about to whisk you to the wedding, I would gobble you all up!'

'Tell your mummy to save some of that deliciousness for me,' Aislin piped up.

'I don't do sharing.'

'Then you won't mind if I eat the giant chocolate bar Dante bought for me all by myself.'

Orla stuck her tongue out at her sister, then felt familiar panic skittle through her veins when the doorbell rang.

That would be Tonino here to collect Finn.

In the month since they'd decided—since *he'd* decided—that they should call time on their relationship, Orla's life had changed immeasurably. For a start, she'd put her Dublin house up for sale and moved in with Aislin and Dante. One thing her time with Tonino had taught her was that she didn't have to do everything alone. She'd thought when Aislin moved to Sicily that she would be fine coping with Finn alone with the medical team on-hand.

She'd been wrong.

She'd been lonely.

She'd proved to herself that she could cope but coping wasn't living.

Tonino had shown her what it was like to live and have fun again. To be a woman, not purely a mother. And, for all Tonino's selflessness, he and Finn deserved to be in each other's lives. Living in Sicily allowed them to spend plenty of time together. It also allowed his family to drop by at all hours to see Finn too. Mercifully, Dante and most of his staff spoke excellent English and translated when needed.

She wouldn't stay with Aislin and Dante for too long. Dante had convinced one of his neighbours that they really wanted to accept an astronomical amount of money for Orla and Finn to buy their home.

Turning to her sister, hoping she would handle the handover as she usually did, she found Aislin with her feet up on the coffee table munching her way through the chocolate bar. She'd hinted darkly a number of times that it was time for Orla to face him alone. She supposed that time was now.

It was fine. She could do it. All she had to do was open the door and wheel Finn to him. Tonino had everything else in hand. She wouldn't have to worry about her son at all. He was never safer and in better care than with his father.

'Come on, Finn,' she said brightly, plastering a smile to her face so big a clown would be envious. One of Tonino's cousins was getting married at his Tuscan hotel. He and Finn and two nurses would fly on his private jet there and stay the night, returning at lunchtime tomorrow.

The smile died when she looked into Tonino's expressionless handsome face and her heart erupted.

He stood at the front door dressed in an identical tuxedo to Finn, the scent of a recent shower and recently applied cologne coming off him in waves.

He nodded at her but avoided her eye. 'All well?'

She nodded back. 'All well.'

'*Bene.* I will see you tomorrow.'

She kissed Finn on the cheek, told him she loved him then stepped back to let Tonino take over.

Another whiff of cologne caught in her senses. A whisper of memory emerged…

Knees suddenly weakening, she pressed herself against the wall by the door.

The missing pieces of her time with Tonino flashed through her retinas with the speed of a bullet.

She *remembered*.

She remembered making love to him. She remembered the first wonderful, tender time. She remembered all the others.

She remembered the abandon. The hedonism. The wantonness. The feeling that what they were sharing together was so wonderful and perfect that it could never be wrong.

The car pulled away. She watched, blurry eyed, until it disappeared from sight, the world only coming back into focus when another memory shot through her brain. The final memory. The last missing piece.

Her heart began to hammer and she put a fist in her mouth to stop herself from howling.

With his baby growing in her belly, she'd cyber-stalked him. She'd cyber-stalked him for *months*, bracing herself for a picture of Tonino and a new lover to appear. When she'd translated the article accompanying the photo of Tonino and Giulia and learned she was his sister, not his lover, Finn had kicked her so hard it had physically hurt. That kick had delivered some much-needed sense into her.

That had been the moment she'd realised she loved Tonino.

She sank to the ground and hugged her knees to her chest as the memories flooded her and the truth she'd hidden from screamed at her.

In her heart, Orla had been waiting for the real Tonino to reveal himself. He'd been too handsome, too sexy and too chivalrous for it to all be true. She'd put him on a pedestal fully expecting him to be knocked off it and knocked off he had been. Sophia's confrontation with her, however much it had sickened her, had almost come as a relief.

Because there was no way a man like Tonino could return her feelings. Her father didn't want her, her mother had abandoned her...why would a man like Tonino want her when he could have any woman in the whole wide world? She'd believed that long before she'd learned he was as rich as Croesus.

But he *had* wanted her! He'd lied about his identity but no one could fake the affection he'd shown her or fake his desire.

Orla had known then that whatever fears she had, she needed to go to him. She'd needed to see him in the flesh and tell him of the life they'd created together. To give him the chance to defend himself, as she should have done from the start. To tell him that she loved him. To see if they could possibly have a future together.

So desperate had she been to get to him that she'd booked a flight online without caring who the carrier was, grabbed her passport and set off to Dublin airport, barely registering the atrocious weather conditions.

She'd been on her way to Tonino.

She remembered slowing to a crawl, intending to pull over when visibility got to less than zero, but the accident itself was a blank. That was one memory she would never get back.

The accident had stopped her getting to the man she loved. She'd failed in her mission to tell him of her love then and she'd failed to tell him that she loved him still because she'd been too scared to see the truth. And now it was all too late.

She'd screwed it all up again.

Hold on a minute…!

What had he said about love and trust the last time they were alone together, the night it had all fallen apart? Hadn't he implied that he loved her?

Could he…?

Tonino had given her every opportunity to see the truth but she'd kept her blinkers on and stayed deliberately blind. In her own blind way she had sabotaged them.

'Are you going to sit here all day?'

Shaken out of the trance she'd fallen into, she looked up to find Aislin in the doorway, still munching on the now depleted bar of chocolate.

Aislin had been scared to love Dante, she remembered. Her insecurities had been acute too.

Their mother had a lot to answer for.

But their mother could not be blamed for Orla's failure to embrace the life Tonino had offered her and which she'd been too frightened to accept.

'Ash?' she whispered.

'Yes?'

'I think I love him.' Then, raising her voice, she said it with conviction. 'I love Tonino.'

Her sister's beautiful face gazed down on her, chewing slowly. Then she swallowed her mouthful and held out a hand to help Orla up. 'Well, took you long enough.'

'What? You knew?'

'Of course I knew, you eejit.' Aislin put her arm around her and held her close as they walked back into the house. It wouldn't be long before Aislin's belly entered the room first. 'Now all you need to decide is what you're going to do about it.'

Do?

She thought quickly, the rudiments of a plan forming.

'Do you think Dante would mind if I borrowed his jet this afternoon?'

'Fancy a trip to Tuscany, do you?' Aislin asked with a grin. 'Are you going to gatecrash the wedding?'

'Something like that.'

'Want some help making yourself look beautiful before you leave?'

'Actually…yes, please.'

Tonino placed a kiss to his exhausted child's forehead. Finn was already asleep. It had been a long day for him and all the playing and dancing with the other children had worn him out.

Leaving him with the duty nurse, Tonino slipped into the adjoining suite and poured himself a bourbon. He needed something stronger than wine and he needed a few minutes to himself before rejoining his family in the ballroom.

The temptation to stay in his suite and bury his troubles in the bottom of the bottle was strong.

He'd been doing well this past month. He'd kept himself busy. He accepted he'd probably drunk a little more wine than was good for him, but a man needed to sleep.

And then this morning Orla had been the one to hand Finn over to him.

He hadn't been prepared for seeing her. Normally she hid away and let Aislin take care of the handover, which had suited him perfectly.

In the past month he and Orla had exchanged dozens of polite messages but until that morning they hadn't seen each other in person or spoken.

Seeing her again had hit him like a punch in the gut.

Had he imagined the misery he'd seen swirling in her green eyes? Had it just been a figment of his imagination, a desperate hope that she might miss him as much as he missed her?

Damn it to hell, he missed her more than he'd believed possible. More than he'd missed her four years ago. And she'd moved to Sicily! That had only made things worse.

She was here in his country but not for him.

He wanted to hate her. If he could turn every ounce of the love he carried in his soul for her into hate, he might feel as if there was a purpose to his life.

Finn was his purpose now. It was everything else that had become meaningless. If not for Finn, he wouldn't have bothered coming to this wedding. He wouldn't have had to put up with Sophia, a guest on the bride's side, glaring at him for the duration.

His father had noticed. He'd leaned into Tonino during the meal and whispered, 'You dodged a bullet there, my son.'

If he'd had the energy to laugh, he would have done. Raucously. Instead, he'd kissed his father's cheek and told him he loved him. And then he'd done the same to his mother. The unspoken rift that had dogged his life these past four years was over. Injured pride had seen him twist their own injured pride into more than it was and blinded him. Their son had dumped their closest friends' daughter without a word of warning and cloistered himself away with a new woman without pausing for breath—of course they'd been embarrassed and angry. That didn't mean they didn't support him. He'd only failed to see it for what it was rather than seeing it as proof that their love was conditional because he'd been in agony over losing Orla.

That agony was nothing compared to the agony of losing her a second time.

Orla was too sick with nerves to care a jot about the magnificent converted monastery whose steps she climbed to enter. She bit back her frustration at having to justify her presence—this was a wedding of two rich, powerful families so security was bound to be tight—by showing her passport and explaining she was the mother of Tonino Valente's child.

The taller of the security guards burst out laughing.

'It's not a joke,' she beseeched, too tired to be affronted. 'Please, let me in.'

When she'd decided to fly to Tuscany and declare herself to Tonino, she'd imagined she would be there in a couple of hours. She hadn't bargained on Aislin spending an age doing her hair and make-up and finding the perfect outfit for her to wear. Then she'd had to wait for a flight-slot out of Sicily, then the helicopter that was supposed to fly her to the wedding had suffered a fault and the pilot had refused to take off so she'd had to wait for a taxi. She would have been happy getting into any old banger but the pilot, who'd organised the taxi for her, was insistent that she wait for an official chauffeured car. She'd had no idea where the official car was coming from—Siberia, maybe?—but after an hour of impatient waiting she'd managed to get through the language barrier and order a taxi for herself. Unfortunately, arriving in an ordinary taxi had meant the security guards looked at her and thought she was ordinary too; far too ordinary to be an invited guest to this society wedding. Especially as she didn't have an invitation.

As her gaze darted around for another way into the hotel, her heart sank to see security guards posted pretty much everywhere.

'Call him,' she pleaded when the tall security guard proved immovable. 'Please, call Mr Valente. He'll vouch for me.'

She was rewarded with another, even heartier laugh.

Salvation came in the unexpected form of Sophia.

The beautiful Sicilian woman appeared from the sprawling gardens and walked up the ancient steps, cat's eyes narrowed, smelling of cigarettes. A conversation in Sicilian broke out between Sophia and the security guard that ended with Sophia taking Orla's arm and dragging her into the hotel, throwing what was obviously a curse over her shoulder at the humiliated security guard.

The only people in the huge hotel reception were teenagers sprawled over the leather sofas escaping their parents to do some serious snogging. One couple broke for air when they walked in but, when they realised it was no one who was going to tell them off, got back to the business at hand.

Sophia dropped her hold on Orla's arm and stepped back to inspect her critically. 'You look...*bene.*'

'Thank you.' Orla braced herself for a scratch down the face. 'And thank you for vouching for me.'

Sophia waved a bored hand. 'I think is too late to see your son—Tonino has taken him to bed.'

Orla nodded. She would find someone who could tell her which one his suite was. Or call one of Finn's nurses. Or she could bite the bullet and actually call Tonino...

'He is beautiful boy.'

'Sorry?'

'Your son.'

'Oh.' Orla waited for the sting in the tail to the compliment. 'Thank you.'

Sophia shifted so she was directly in front of Orla, forcing Orla to brace herself again for attack. The Sicilian woman looked her up and down one last time before her haughty, beautiful face softened. Then she did something that stunned Orla completely. Sophia wrapped her bony arms around her and pulled her into an even bonier embrace.

'I am sorry,' Sophia whispered in her ear, even while she actively avoided a single strand of their hair touching. Then she pulled away, squeezed Orla's hands with a rueful, apologetic smile, turned on her heel and clip-clopped into the ballroom.

Tonino tipped another hefty measure of bourbon down his neck. This one, he was sure, would numb his aching heart. His intention to leave the suite and join the wedding reception for another hour had come to nothing.

Pinching the bridge of his nose, he breathed in deeply.

He did not think there was a place he would less like to be than at the reception party celebrating the marriage of another happy couple when he felt so raw inside.

What was Orla doing? Sitting with her sister watching a movie and sharing a large bowl of popcorn? Or had she gone to bed already? Did she have one of those headaches she suffered from? If he drank enough of this bourbon would he have a matching headache, or would it just send him to sleep?

It was while he was debating the merits of drinking until he passed out—Finn was fast asleep and under the nurse's watchful care—that the knock on his door came.

He rubbed the nape of his neck with a sigh.

Another knock quickly followed.

Figuring it was likely to be his mother hoping for another kiss with her grandson, he got grudgingly to his feet.

When he saw who was there he was so certain it was an alcohol-induced hallucination that he laughed mirthlessly at the fertility of his imagination and shut the door in the mirage's face.

He took two steps back to the sofa and his bottle of bourbon and froze.

His hands were shaking. His legs were shaking. His heart was pumping harder than he had ever felt it pump before.

He spun back and took the two steps needed to reach the door again and fling it open.

It was no mirage.

The woman standing at the door, ravishing in a green silk halter-neck dress, thick dark hair lightly curled into waves, clearly apprehensive behind the sultry make-up, was Orla.

As if in a dream, Tonino stepped wordlessly aside and admitted her into his suite.

Her divine scent followed her inside, clinging to her like a cloud and diving straight into his bloodstream to make his heart thump even harder.

Orla had never felt such a mixture of terror and excitement as she had when she'd knocked on Tonino's door. To have it slammed straight back shut again had stunned her and she'd just plucked up the courage to knock again when he opened it a second time looking as if he'd seen a ghost.

And that was when all the terror left her.

The desolation and fighting wonder in Tonino's eyes crowded out the lingering doubt. He did love her. She felt it as deeply as she felt their son's love.

'Orla…?'

She stepped to him and placed a finger gently to his mouth. Their gazes held for a long, lingering moment. Then she took hold of his hand and silently led him into the bedroom.

She waited until he was sitting on thc bcd bcfore breaking the hold of their hands and stepping back.

He didn't say a word, just gazed at her, his breaths taut and shallow.

She'd come to his suite without a plan, without any rehearsed speech, her only intent being to find him. Now that she was here she knew what she had to do. What she *must* do.

Saying a prayer for courage first, she drew the curtains. Then she dimmed the lights so the only illumination was a soft glow. It was enough for him to see.

The dress she wore had one button at the nape of her neck. Standing only a few steps from Tonino, she undid it. The dress held for a moment before falling to her waist. Keeping her eyes fixed on the man she loved, she reached round to her back and pulled the small zip down so the entire dress fell to her feet, leaving her naked except for a pair of black lace knickers and the heeled shoes she now stepped out of.

Then she pulled the knickers down, stepped out of them too and walked to him, certain he must be able to see her heart beating frantically beneath her chest.

There was a boulder-like lump in Tonino's throat. It was the only thing stopping his heart from flying out of his mouth.

Was he dreaming? He hardly dared move a muscle in case he woke from it.

She stood between his parted thighs and reached for his hand. Her touch felt real. When she placed it on her stomach… That felt real too.

He exhaled everything in his lungs then re-filled them. Orla's scent merged with the air he breathed in.

He closed his eyes and counted to ten. When he opened them, she was still there, a look in her eyes that made his hammering heart swell.

Slowly, he allowed his gaze to drift down her body.

Pregnancy had changed it only a little since he'd last seen her naked. Her breasts were fuller, the nipples darker. Her hips were a little wider, her stomach more rounded. And slashed across that same stomach were two long, vivid scars, one vertical, the other horizontal…and as he looked he found another, smaller horizontal scar across her knicker-line. There were numerous different smaller scars too, marring her chest and the tops of her arms. Scars from where shards of glass had penetrated her skin.

In the blurred recess of his mind came the realisation that the dress she'd just stripped out of had exposed her arms. He'd been too busy staring in wonder at the mirage of her appearance to notice.

She pivoted slowly to show him her back. More scars.

Something hot stabbed the backs of his eyes, something so unexpected and rare that it took a few beats before Tonino recognised it as tears.

Placing his hands on her hips, he pressed his cheek against her back, closed his eyes and breathed her in. He felt her tremble.

Then she turned again and cupped his face with her hands. Bringing her face close to his, she stared deep into his brimming eyes.

'You make me feel things that terrify me,' she whispered before brushing her mouth against his and moving her hands from his face to trail down his neck and unbutton his shirt.

Her lips found his neck and bit it gently while her hand found the button of his trousers.

A shudder shot through him.

Between brushes of lips and darts of tongue she continued. 'My feelings for you scared me so much four years ago that I took the first opportunity to run.' She pulled the zip of his trousers down and tugged them to his hips. 'I didn't trust my feelings for you, and I didn't trust your feelings for me.'

'Orla…'

Her name came as a groan from his mouth, but no further words came for she'd covered his mouth with her own again and whispered a soft, 'Shh.'

Mouths fused, she pushed gently at his chest so he was lying on the bed.

Parting his shirt, she ran her hands over his chest before shifting to straddle him, elbows either side of his face, green eyes boring into his. 'I cannot express how sorry I am. I was a frightened rabbit. That day…that rejection from my father and then that confrontation with Sophia…' She kissed the tip of his nose. 'They were the confirmation I needed that you weren't to be trusted and that I should run. I didn't give you a chance to defend yourself and I will regret that for the rest of my life. My only defence is that I was terrified. Most of the people I love have rejected me. My father didn't want me. My mother never wanted me… How could you want me?' She squeezed her eyes shut before reaching down to tug his trousers and underwear lower still, freeing his erection. 'Do you remember leaving for Tuscany? You kissed me goodbye and said that we needed to talk that night. After what Sophia told me, I thought you were going to tell me it was over. I ran before I could be pushed.'

'I was going to tell you the truth,' he said quietly, sincerity and pain ringing in his eyes. 'And then I was going to ask you to marry me.'

Her chin wobbled. A tear fell from her eye and landed on his cheek. 'I'm sorry for everything. I'm sorry for realising my feelings too late. If I hadn't been such a coward you would have been there for the pregnancy and the birth. Everything would have been different. The accident wouldn't have happened…'

'Hey.' Gripping her wrists, he used his strength to flip Orla onto her back so that he was the one straddling her before she could protest. 'Don't you dare blame yourself for that. It was not your fault.'

More tears leaked from her eyes, falling onto the pillow beneath her head. 'I was coming to you.'

'What?'

'That day. The accident. I was going to the airport. I was coming to find you. To tell you about the baby and to tell you…'

'Tell me what?' he whispered when her voice became too choked for words to form.

She swallowed but did not move her glistening eyes from his. 'That the only happiness I have ever truly known has been with you. I love you. I loved you then and I love you now. I do want to marry you, Tonino. Not for Finn's sake but for mine because living without you is hell. I'm lost. I've been lost and searching for you for four years. I love you and if there is any chance you love me and still see a future for us, I will take it and I will fight for it. I will fight for you and I will fight for us. I love you.'

Orla, purged of all the things she had needed to say, felt her chest fill with dread as Tonino remained silent.

And then he smiled and blinked back what looked suspiciously like his own tears. 'Orla O'Reilly…' He closed his eyes and kissed her reverently. 'My love, you cannot know how badly I have wanted to hear those words from you. What happened four years ago… I think we can both share blame for that. I should have told you the truth of who I was, but I was a coward who was scared that you would change and become like all the other women in my world.' He brushed away a strand of hair that had fallen over her face. 'I never imagined that someone like you existed and when you disappeared it was like the darkest shadow had settled over

EPILOGUE

ORLA STOOD OUTSIDE the Bally House church doors and looked up at the blue sky with a smile.

'Thank you,' she whispered to whoever was out there listening to these things. Whoever that deity was, she would be for ever grateful for them turning the sun on over her beautiful Emerald Isle for this one day.

Her sister gave her one last critical inspection before a huge smile broke over her face. 'You look beautiful,' she said, eyes brimming.

Orla punched her in the arm. 'Pack it in or you'll get me going.'

Aislin sniffed and blinked frantically. 'I'm sorry. Stupid hormones.'

Dante, who was hovering behind the two sisters, coughed loudly.

'Don't you make that noise, sir,' Aislin told him sternly. 'It's your fault I'm so hormonal.'

If Dante were a peacock his tail would be in full bloom.

me. I never settled down because I couldn't. You had taken my heart with you.'

Orla felt that she could choke from all the emotion filling her. She pressed her lips to his, needing the closeness, needing to feel his breath and the warmth of his touch like a bee seeking pollen.

Somehow, in the weight of the tender kiss they shared, he slid his trousers off and rested himself between her legs.

Incredible sensations suffused her as he drove slowly inside her.

'I love you, Orla,' he whispered raggedly as he withdrew to the tip. 'I fell in love with you so quickly I didn't even know it was happening. I tried to forget you, but it was impossible. You were in my head and in my heart, and you have never left it. My love is yours for ever.'

And then he thrust deep inside her.

Orla wrapped her arms tightly around his neck and her legs tightly around his waist and, lips crushed together, succumbed to the heady pulsations growing in intensity in her slavish body and filling into her heart so that when she reached her climax and the pulsations ripped through her very being, her heart opened like a flower in bloom and never closed again.

Orla rolled her eyes. Fair enough, he was proud that he was going to be a father again, but the strutting peacock act was wearing pretty thin, especially when her own belly was starting to resemble a watermelon. In this respect fate had proved to have an evil sense of humour, with Orla discovering she was pregnant the day after they'd sent all the wedding invitations out. That would teach them not to use contraception. She didn't know who'd been happier about the pregnancy—her, Tonino or Finn.

'Are you going to walk me down the aisle or what?'

Her brother laughed and took her arm. Aislin giggled and helped Finn to his feet. She would hold his hand every step of the walk down the aisle behind his mummy, for which Finn was determined to carry his parents' wedding rings.

Giulia, Tonino's sister, and the four children on Tonino's side old enough to follow Orla down the aisle without trying to make a run for it, took their positions behind the train of her dress.

Inside the church, the organist struck up the wedding march.

The two hundred guests, Sicilians and Irish alike out in force, craned their heads, a buzz of excitement permeating the musty chapel air.

At the top of the aisle stood Tonino, supported by his brother. On the front row to the right were his parents and three surviving grandparents. On the front row to the left were Dante's mother and his latest stepfather. Strangely, Orla had found herself forging the unlikeliest of bonds with the woman whose marriage Orla's conception had destroyed. Immacolata had Aislin and Dante's six-month-old son Sal standing on her lap. Orla bit her cheeks to hide the laughter when she witnessed Sal dribble into an oblivious Immacolata's immaculately groomed and glossy hair.

The warmth from everyone crammed in the church filled her heart and for a moment she had to blink back tears.

This was it. This was the moment she and Tonino officially pledged their lives together, and, as she looked into the dark chocolate eyes of the man she loved so much and recited the vows that would tie her to him for ever, she knew he was thinking exactly what she was thinking.

That nothing would ever come between them again.

* * * * *

1507

ReaderService.com has a new look!

We have refreshed our website and we want to share our new look with you. Head over to ReaderService.com and check it out!

On ReaderService.com, you can:

- Try 2 free books from any series
- Access risk-free special offers
- View your account history & manage payments
- Browse the latest Bonus Bucks catalog

Don't miss out!

If you want to stay up-to-date on the latest at the Reader Service and enjoy more Harlequin content, make sure you've signed up for our monthly News & Notes email newsletter. Sign up online at ReaderService.com.

RS19